INFERNAL AFFAIRS

SAINT TOMMY, NYPD BOOK 3

DECLAN FINN

DEATH CULT

SAINT TOMMY, NYPD BOOK TWO

By Declan Finn

Published by Silver Empire

https://silverempire.org/

Cover by Steve Beaulieu

❀ Created with Vellum

Dedicated to Kathleen McGauran, who introduced me to new places to destroy in New Jersey.

Chapter 1

MARTYR AND SAINT

A martyr is a title in the Catholic church for saints who died for their faith. It was a title I never expected to have.

As I sat in the front row, side seat of my church, Saint Gregory the Great, it occurred to me that the above title would be slapped upon my tombstone only as the bullets started to fly.

Father Jerome Delaney, the celebrant, was the first to be shot. The sharp *crack* of the rifle echoed through as he started to talk about how God was and is Love. He shuddered with the impact as the five bullets punched into his chest and fell back with the last bullet, which was impressive for a man as old as he had been. He was dead before he hit the floor.

My family and I were seated to the right of the altar as you faced the altar. We were less interested in being seen in the front and more interested in being in a position to drown out the guitarist on the other side of the altar from us with our singing. We weren't good, but we were mildly in tune, unlike the guitar, or the cantor.

I was with Mariel, my wife, and Jeremy, my son. Mariel had long, wavy chestnut brown hair, round, deep-brown eyes, a pleasant heart-shaped face, and a healthy olive complexion. As Ben Franklin would say, we fit well together. Jeremy was eleven, energetic, and ... very much an 11-year-old boy.

When the first shot went off, I dropped to one knee and reached for my handgun. My wife Mariel bent over to protect our unborn daughter. Our son Jeremy crouched so low he was nearly under the seats.

"Plan 22 C," I said.

Both of them nodded. Ever since the serial killer had broken into our home, we had come up with a collection of contingency plans.

Plan C was always "run while I lay down cover fire."

Before they could even get off the floor, I jumped onto the back of the chair in front of me. It tilted forward, and I jumped onto the next chair before it fell forward. I leaped to the small rail for climbing up on the altar -- it had been installed for those who couldn't do steps without holding onto something - and then took a giant leap to the center.

I went for the top of the altar for multiple reasons: first, visibility, and second, I wanted to be the biggest, clearest target. Thank God none of the paraphernalia for later in Mass was there yet.

The shooter was at the back of the church, rifle held high. Since the first shot, everyone in the church stood and ran. Few had ducked to cover-—along with those who had merely tripped those trying to run.

And half the church had run directly into the center aisle, in front of the shooters.

I dropped to one knee, gun up and ready. I grabbed the microphone from the altar and bellowed, "Freeze! Police!"

The rifle man turned and swung his muzzle up to aim for me.

Better than aiming at the congregation.

I aimed high and fired. The first bullet scraped along the barrel of the rifle, catching the ejector, and drilling into his shoulder. It turned him around before a round went off. He nearly decapitated a statue of the Virgin Mary. The second bullet struck up just right of center mass (his right, not mine). My third bullet missed by a hair, scoring him across the forehead.

The shooter's rifle came down. He staggered back and grabbed his arm. He slumped up against the side of a pew, grabbed his rifle with his good hand, and raised the barrel to aim again.

I fired again, catching him in the breast, right beneath the clavicle. He leaned straight back this time and went down.

The only way to get to him would have been through the horde of church goers. I frowned, thought it over a moment, and prayed a little.

I pushed forward in a leap ... that was aided by a little divine intervention. The levitation trick that I prayed for was just enough to leap from the altar to the front pew. I leaped from the back of the pew to the one behind it. I continued like that from one pew to another, looking like a parkour runner. I wasn't thinking at the time, giving only a brief thought to how I would explain this if anyone had noticed——God's little parlor trick.

I leaped off once the crowd had petered out, landing in the aisle.

This also put me in direct line of sight of the shooter.

His muzzle came up a few inches and pulled the trigger.

It clicked.

The shooter looked as confused as I felt. I lunged forward and kicked the rifle away from him. The rifle had been damaged. My first bullet jammed the ejector, and the last spent casing did not eject.

The shooter was a walking cliché: socialist, hammer and sickle badge, Che Guevara shirt.

The shooter smiled at me and laughed. "Almost got you, you capitalist pig. You won't be lucky next time."

There was a burst of bullets from outside. My head shot up. The automatic gunfire was unlike the shooter I just dropped. I darted out of the back of the vestibule (away from the altar), then through the front door of the church.

Outside. The church was empty of people. Since I didn't trust to locate the gunfire by sound alone (directionality of sound can be a pain in the butt), I turned right. Because there had been an active shooter in the church, and no one had appeared from the nearby police car parked near the entrance behind the altar side of the church.

I turned around the corner. Four men with M4 rifles were hosing down the three men crouched behind the patrol car. I charged the gunmen. They didn't turn. I was within thirty feet of them when I opened fire. I emptied the magazine into two of the shooters.

The empty magazine ejected from the pistol as I came within arm's reach of the remaining two shooters. I hammered my pistol behind the ear of the shooter on the left. His head bounced off the rear windshield he was hiding behind. A second later, I crashed into the shooter on the right. I crushed the shooter between my shoulder and the side of an SUV. I drove my elbow into the shooter's ear, and then pistol-whipped him. I went back and forth with my pistol, smacking it against the skull of each gunman in turn until they fell down.

I kicked aside the weapons, reloaded my pistol, then took two steps back, covering them. I called out, "Clear! NYPD! Plain clothes!"

Why didn't they even consider sending in more than one guy to the church? I wondered. I immediately answered myself. *Because I'm one guy going to Mass versus being ambushed by two armed cops. Duh.*

Chapter 2

EVERYBODY KNOWS
YOUR NAME

When my partner, Alex Packard, arrived, the party was already in full swing. The entire church had been sealed off, as had the surrounding block. This was especially fun when you consider that the road to one side of the church was the southbound service road for the Cross Island Expressway.

Alex strode in the front door of the church and up the stairs into the vestibule, now called the gathering space for reasons that surpassed all understanding. My family and I were on a bench in the corner, and he came right for us. He sat on the bench going at right angles to ours, leaned back, and smiled.

Alex was a slender, older man. He had an odd pot-belly in the middle of all of that skinny. It was probably from years of booze, but I wasn't going to inquire too closely. I had never seen him take a drink. I only knew about his former drinking problem from a demon, who had been psyching him out at the time. His suit was gray and rumpled, just like he was. He was balding on top, with a graying mustache that Tom Selleck would have approved of. He carried a large paper bag.

"Really?" Alex asked. "Your wife is pregnant. You're with your kid

—hey, Jeremy—and you're in *church*. Church, Tommy. Can't you take even *one* day off?"

With my arm around Mariel's shoulders, I gave him a half-shrug. "They find me. They always find me."

Alex smirked. He shook his head. "No kidding."

"I'm really not." I explained the last words from the first gunman.

Alex winced. "No surprise."

"Yeah!" Jeremy exclaimed excitedly. His voice dropped to a whisper that only mommy, daddy, and Uncle Alex could hear. "Because Daddy's a superhero! They're always going to find him."

Isn't that an encouraging thought? I pondered.

Alex merely smiled at Jeremy. "Kinda, Jerry." He looked back to me. "I ran into Sarge on the way in. She handed me a nice little starter package for you."

Alex raised the paper bag. He reached in and pulled out individual items, explaining each as he went along. Everything was in clear evidence bags, sealed with the red tape of the NYPD Crime Scene Unit. Father Delaney had already been wheeled out.

"They went through the shooter's pockets," Alex said as he went through the bag. "We had these." The first item was a large evidence bag that even could have held the contents of Mariel's purse. "Antipsychotics by the truckload. I'm actually surprised he could walk upright."

Alex placed it down on the bench next to him and grabbed the next bag. This one looked like the contents of his wallet. "Membership cards. He was a registered Demoncrat, as though we couldn't tell from the Che T-shirt and that he was trying to shoot up a church."

I smiled despite myself. Alex had taken to referring to anyone on the Left as a 'Demoncrat' ever since a demon-possessed serial killer who worked for the Women's Health Corps tried to kill us—and after we discovered that the WHC itself was, in reality, a front for a Moloch-worshiping Death Cult. After a while, it did seem that evil had a particular political affiliation.

I had little problem with him saying it because he had genuine cause for a grudge. As most of New York City either voted Democrat or just didn't vote, I was a touch more reluctant to brand all of them with the same demonic brush.

Then again, discussing much of the fallout from the WHC incident was another conversation.

"And," Alex continued, "here's the *fun* part." He pulled out a smaller bag. This one clearly showed a large newspaper clipping. It was one photo—me, from nearly a year ago, during the incident with said demon. I didn't know which headline it was under. It may have been the one who framed my arrest of the perp as Saint versus psycho or the one that claimed I framed an innocent abortionist because I was a Catholic.

"He really was there for you," Alex explained. "Just you. We don't have anything speaking to why."

Mariel scoffed at that. "Maybe he was employed by LaBitch?" she asked, referring to the former head of the Women's Health Corps that Mariel had personally pushed into a fire pit. "Or the Mayor? Or maybe he's a dirty commie and just doesn't like high-profile Catholics like Tommy?"

I frowned. I opened my mouth to dispute that ... and gave up before I started. While I had spent most of my life trying to keep my head down and out of the public eye, the last year had been filled with enough various high-profile incidents that if I had caught the eye of some nut cases online, they would have had little trouble tracking my career.

"Lucky for me," I said, "I moved after that article was published." There were two reasons for that. One, the property damage caused the local village committee to drive us out of the private neighborhood. Two, the newspaper article that picture had been taken from had come complete with my home address. The newspaper had issued a non-apology, but the damage had been done, and we moved a little over eight months ago.

Unfortunately, someone had my home address and had had sent zombies to my house shortly thereafter.

"'Lucky' isn't the term I'd use," Alex said. He shrugged. "But that's not my problem. My problem is they may hit me by accident." He slid the evidence back into the bag. "For the record, the first shooter, the one in the church, is connected to very little, unless we think the entire Communist community is out to get Nolan."

I chuckled. "In that case, time to arrest Columbia University."

Alex rolled his eyes. "Funny."

I frowned. "No. Not really. Especially considering the number of people they murdered last century."

Alex laughed. "Columbia or Communists?"

Mariel nudged me with the crown of her head. "Is there a difference?"

I looked to Alex. "When you say Communist ...?"

"I mean that he's a card-carrying commie. He has cards in his wallet for the party, for Anti-Fa."

I winced. I had never had a personal encounter with them, but I had read enough to know I didn't like them very much. For a group claiming to be "anti-fascist," they were amazingly, well, fascist. Their tactics ranged from violence against people they disagreed with (which was anyone to the right of Mao and Stalin) to ... even more violence against property. They had operated in Europe, beginning as anarchist Communists ... because orderly Communism was bad, surely *chaotic* Communism would be even better? If you can't take over a government-- or in the case of Russia *keep* one – maybe destroying it all would be progress? The European version of the moment hated Catholics ... *Quelle surprise.*

"We know that it wasn't an actual Anti-fa attack," I said. "They tend to swarm. We would have had a few dozen raiding the church just to rip me apart. It might have even worked."

Alex frowned. He was probably considering the various and sundry abilities I possess, running the odds of which would be the best option for going up against a riot. After putting down an entire prison riot by myself the previous year, surely a bunch of local thugs wouldn't be a problem for me.

I wasn't going to explain, yet again, that I wasn't a superhero. While I exhibited some of the miraculous abilities usually attributed to saints, they weren't something that I could take for granted—or even explain why they were given me. The powers came from God, not from me. I wasn't a comic book superhero, no matter what Alex or Jeremy insisted. Jeremy had a good excuse. He was ten.

At least, Jeremy knew better.

"Dad couldn't do anything!" he exclaimed. "Too many witnesses. Do you want to bust his secret identity?"

Mariel and I smiled while Alex shifted uncomfortably. "Yeah. Well, it would be hard to fit into a DD5 report. But that's why I write them up when that happens."

I said nothing, but said a silent thank you prayer to God that I hadn't needed any of the fancier abilities that He had graced me with. While I still smelled out evil on a day-to-day basis, there had been no need to be in two places at once, levitate, drink poison, or heal deadly wounds. Considering the circumstances I was in, I would be perfectly happy if I never needed those abilities. Though to be honest, I was a little surprised that it had taken this long for a situation to arise again. I had gotten into so many firefights, I had a reputation. The calm between storms had been so long, I hadn't been called "Wyatt Earp" in nearly a week.

So much for that going away.

"I'm told that the Bishop's not too happy with the whole thing."

I winced. That was something I didn't want to deal with: Church politics. "Of course he's not. He's going to have to reconsecrate the church." I sighed. "Can we leave now? Didn't eat breakfast before we came."

Alex shrugged. "I hear you. At least, there's one good thing: you won't be investigating what's left. With any luck, this will be an isolated incident. The first shooter was just another in a long line of Demoncrat shooters."

My brows arched. The secondary shooters had had M4 automatic weapons, ready to take out cops and a full church to get to me.

Alex sighed. "Yeah. I know. I don't believe it either."

Chapter 3

SWATED

The rest of the day went normally. The schedule was normal: Church, breakfast, parish activity *du jour*, early dinner, and Jeremy goes to play with his friends, while Mariel and I play with each other...

What? How else did you think Mariel became pregnant?

Ironically, it was Jeremy's recently found fame that allowed for Mariel's current condition. After facing down a serial killer and being kidnapped by a deranged death cult, Jeremy had become a source of fascination for his classmates. This led to a lot of busy weekends of fun for Jeremy, and lots of privacy for us.

Remember, when Catholics get married, part of the marriage contract is to contribute to the gene pool as much as possible.

By nine o'clock that evening, we were all ready to sleep.

There is a reason that the first words of every angel in the Bible tend to be "Be not afraid."

That is because angels of the Lord are totally *terrifying*.

In my dream, the body was made of fire. The wings looked like butterfly wings, taller and wider than the main body. And it looked like a Kaiju that would make Godzilla crawl back into the sea and ask directions for the Marianas Trench. Its sword was a cross between a big broadsword and a lightsaber, and big enough to cleave the world in half.

When it told me to Be Not Afraid, it sounded musical and lyrical and at total odds with the creature in front of me.

"Thomas Nolan! Judge and Prophet of the Lord! Awake and smite the agents of Satan!"

I was out of bed, on my feet, with a gun in my hand before I knew I was awake.

I turned and violently shook Mariel awake. Her eyes snapped open, and she reached for her side table, then hesitated when she recognized me. At least, she hadn't shanked me with the flip knife at her side.

I told her, simply, "One-A."

It was the plan for her to hunker down and wait in Jeremy's room —mostly because his room's door opened almost straight into the staircase. Anyone who came up the stairs would get to the second landing, turn left, and go up four more steps.

She got up and grabbed her rifle, next to her side table. She slung the strap over her head, then grabbed the shotgun, next to the rifle. Then she grabbed her pistol and held it in her other hand. I did the same, mostly to horde the weapons as they hunkered down.

We were, after a fashion, preppers. Mostly because after the first two home invasions by supernatural and demonic forces, we came prepared.

I led the way as Mariel carried the weapons behind her. I waited until she was in Jeremy's room, then handed her the shotgun. I left the rifle slung over my shoulder, and carried the pistol in hand. It was a Browning Hi-Powered. It wasn't exactly department issue, but I had started a collection of larger caliber guns since the death cult came for us.

I took the stairs carefully and quietly. I took one step down from the top landing when the door crashed in. I dropped to a crouch and waited. I didn't scream out a warning, since I didn't want to give away my position. And since the front door was made of metal, just kicking the door in wasn't an option, so they weren't simple home invaders.

Also, I was told to *smite the agents of Satan*, so I could only conclude that these dirt bags weren't here to play.

They swept in like a well-oiled machine, a snake-like line of men carrying body armor and rifles. The first one looked up at me—directly at me, I'm certain—and whispered, "Clear."

The leader moved the muzzle down and ahead.

I waited until I could clearly see the tail end of this serpent. There were only six of them.

After the third one moved into the living room and broke to their left (heading towards our dining room), the fourth one stepped into the living room and moved for the steps.

That's when I opened fire. The first bullet slammed into the armored helmet, slamming the man's head into the wall. The second round punched through the man's neck. He collapsed without a sound, but I had already moved onto the next man in order. I took a step back, onto the landing, as I fired again. Both bullets found their mark, though not the way I wanted. One bullet merely collided with the Kevlar vest—but the force of the round cracked the collar bone. The next one punched under the arm, into the armpit, and pinballed around through the rib cage, caged inside by Kevlar.

The third one turned his attention to me, and I triple-tapped him. Three rounds from the Hi-Power knocked him back, and he involuntarily opened fire with a string of bullets that cut right above my head. I dove up the stairs, getting out of the line of sight and line of fire.

I scrambled up the stairs. I swung around the wall at the top of the stairs. I dropped back to a crouch. The were well-armed, and had good tactics. The first thing I could think of was: *We're screwed. Dear Lord. We'll need some help here.*

There were stomps as one of them charged up the stairs. I was ready to intercept them as soon as they appeared. But after only eight steps, they stopped. I couldn't figure out why for a second.

Then I heard the distinct metallic scrape of a pin being pulled out of a grenade.

The instant the next attacker leaned over to aim, I fired twice. His arm had been up and ready to hurl his device. The helmet's visor cracked, and his head snapped back with the bullet. The second bullet punched into his wrist, shattering it. He fell back with a scream, and so did his grenade. There were a few gasps from down below once they realized what had happened.

I ducked back and covered my ears. Which was a good idea, because the explosion was bright and loud enough to make your eyes and ears bleed if you were too close.

Thankfully for my home, it was a flash bang, not a fragmentation or incendiary.

Since I only had two bullets left, I unslung my rifle and darted across Mariel's line of fire for the little room leading up to the attic. We hadn't decided what else to do with it yet, so it was still filled with boxes of random stuff we still hadn't unpacked yet.

We all waited for a long moment, listening intently. The next one up came up quietly. Mariel hadn't waited for the gunman to notice her. His helmet appeared, and she fired three times. His helmet snapped to one side. His head crashed into the window on the second landing.

It was followed by multiple rounds of blind fire in automatic bursts. Mariel rolled out of the way of the gunfire. This fifth gunman fired off a few rounds every step, keeping Mariel back.

I waited as he came up, one step at a time, one burst at a time. I pressed myself against the wall, I almost felt him coming closer.

Then I heard the slide of an empty magazine ejecting from the gun and thumping on the floor.

I wheeled around the doorway before the gunman had even had a chance to grab a fresh magazine. I jammed the muzzle of my Browning underneath the man's chin and pulled the trigger twice, firing the last two bullets. The brain and bone spattered out of the helmet ...

And into the visor of the gunman right behind him.

Oh Nuts.

I dropped the pistol and brought up my rifle. It collided with the rifle of the other gunman, and he smashed into me. He drove me into the room of junk, slamming me into the door. The gunman reared back with his right fist. I jerked my head to one side, and he punched the wall. He cursed.

I twisted with my rifle counter-clockwise as I twisted my body the same way. The butt of my AR-15 cracked against the gunman's helmet while I slipped out of the way. I shoved off of the gunman and raised my rifle.

The gunman spun. He smacked the muzzle of my rifle off line as he raised his own. I raised my knee as high as I could, then kicked down at the muzzle of his gun, shoving it to the floor. As my foot came down, I reared forward, shoving my left forearm into his throat.

I jammed my rifle down into the boot of the gunman, then fired. He screamed. My left forearm was still in his throat. I drove my elbow into the helmet, forcing him to look to my left. My fingers found the back of his helmet, hooking underneath it. I spun to my left and dragged the gunman down by his helmet, throwing him off the wall. He didn't go far, so I didn't raise my rifle level with him. I raised the muzzle just enough to shoot him in the back of the knee. He screamed and fell forward, away from me.

My rifle came up, and I fired. I didn't even count the bullets I fired into him. I only stopped pulling the trigger when he went down.

I took a slow, deep breath.

I swung around. "Mariel, don't shoot. I'm crossing your field of fire."

I moved into the hall, then down the stairs. I cleared the house in less than a minute. I lowered my gun about the time that the sirens rang outside. I placed the gun down and started turning on the lights, keeping at least one hand up at all times. I knew the uniforms that arrived, one of them was Sgt. Mary Russell.

Russell stood in the doorway between the enclosed front porch and the living room, stopping before the first body. She looked down at the body, then at me. She considered me, then shrugged. "Nice boxers."

I rolled my eyes. "Gee. Thanks."

She laughed as she shook her head and holstered her gun. She looked over the bodies. "Dang, Wyatt. Don't you have quiet days?"

I narrowed my eyes. "It's been quiet for *months*."

Her eyebrows went up, and smiled. "Twice in one day, though? At least, you're making up for lost time."

I sighed. "Apparently."

She looked down at the corpse, and I did as well. The Kevlar was strange, mainly because there was black masking tape on it... and the helmet. I glanced to the other corpses in the room and on the stairs. The masking tape was on all of them.

What the?

I stepped forward and crouched down by the nearest corpse. I reached over to the edge of the masking tape, gently teasing the tape over. I only needed a corner to come off. It revealed the upper corner of a letter: S.

"Crud."

Russell said, "What's the matter?"

I rose, and started to work my way up the stairs. "I'm getting dressed. Call the LT. Call the Captain. Then call Statler and Waldorf over at IA."

"Why?" she called after me.

I stopped on the second landing, around the corpse under the window. "Tell them that the people who tried to kill me are members of a SWAT team."

Russell gave me a long look. "Congratulations. I guess you're a cop killer."

Chapter 4

PICKING UP THE PIECES

The SWAT team had invaded my home at two in the morning. By 2:30, the neighbors were awake, and it looked like my station house was having a block party on my street. The SWAT van the team had arrived in was parked around the corner, so the entire intersection would be blocked off until the scene was processed. Ten patrol cars were used just to secure the area. CSU was already there in record time, and they weren't happy that Mariel, Jeremy, and I had already walked all over the crime scene, since it was mostly on our staircase.

CSU took photos of me and Mariel, then confiscated our sleep-wear. They collected rug fibers from the front of Mariel's night shirt to prove that she had been on the floor (As she said, "I didn't even get to shoot someone, but I still need to sacrifice my clothing? Not fair."). They took my clothing since I had blood spatter on it. We were already informed that parts of the carpet on our staircase would be taken away because of the burns from the flash bang. We were processed before the rest of the crime scene, and we needed to get dressed for the day.

Jeremy hadn't been involved, except in making the 911 call and another call to the station. He was already asleep on the couch. After being threatened at knife point by a serial killer, and kidnapped by a cult with its own Voodoo man, this was relatively boring. I was half afraid that when puberty hit my son, he was going to turn into a thrill-seeking adrenaline junkie. I could see a lot of ER visits in our future.

My Captain was there not long after CSU finished with us. My Lieutenant barely beat him to it. Both were in full dress uniforms, as though they were showing up to a full-court press conference, or to a funeral. I didn't relish either prospect. They sat at the opposite end of the table while Mariel sat at the other. She had been making coffee since the coast was clear. They were all disposable cups, purchased after one of the last CSU guys broke a cup the last time the house had been a crime scene.

Then Alex Packard showed up. My partner burst in through the front door barely dressed. He wore loafers with no socks. His gray slacks were buckled, the fly only half up. The buttons on his shirt were misaligned, but he'd given up on the top two buttons, so it didn't matter. His bright yellow tie was draped over his neck, untied. What was left of his hair stuck up at all sorts of odd angles.

"Tommy! Don't say a thing!" Alex called. "I'm your PBA rep, and I insist—"

I held up a hand. He stopped raving for a moment as he stopped at the dining room table. He grabbed the edge, and panted heavily. "Sorry. I ran. A lot. Gotta never do that again."

I restrained myself from rolling my eyes. "Now that you're here, we can start."

Alex started to object. "Tommy—"

I lifted a tablet from the seat next to me. It was normally Jeremy's, which is why the case was black with an Alex Ross rendering of *The Shadow* on the back. I tapped into the house WiFi, then turned it around to my superiors and my partner.

Mariel left to go to the kitchen. She'd been here for the next part.

It was a full audio-video of the entire attack. The cameras on the front porch, the stairs, and the upper hallway caught every last moment. Not once did anyone hear the word "Police!" or "Freeze!"

The only verbal communication was between Mariel and me. Everything between the officers was communicated purely in hand gestures.

When the recording was over, both of my superiors looked pissed off. They said nothing, and I didn't blame them. Officially, Internal Affairs should be the one to talk to me right now, not them.

Right now, they were in an awkward position. Both of my superiors were facing a nightmare scenario and doing the math on which was worse.

1: Headline, "THOMAS NOLAN MURDERS SIX COPS." This is the headline that wins a cold shoulder from everyone in the department and even future backup to "arrive too late" to a full shootout.

2: Headline, "SWAT TEAM TRIES TO KILL SAINTLY COP." This headline gets every cop in the department to buy me beers for getting them before they got me. Meanwhile, this also puts every cop in the city under a magnifying glass, especially the department out of which SWAT operated.

3: Headline, "COP ON COP VIOLENCE: EVERYONE WINS." This makes for a police department that closes ranks and acts amazingly cranky to the entire population.

This didn't even count what "Hizzonor" the Mayor, Ricardo Hoynes, would do.

Hoynes was already against cops in general, and me in particular. Given that his Deputy Mayor for Social Justice Programs was a zombie-raising Voodoo Bokor who had tried to murder me a few months back, I could count on hearing a few tasteful sound bites from the mayor during this entire ordeal.

Whether or not Deputy Mayor Bokor Baracus (yes, this particular demonic presence was that subtle) was just using the Mayor to further a Satanic agenda, or if the Mayor was the greater darkness, was unknown. Even my ability to smell evil was useless around City Hall—there was so much evil in the air, it was impossible to get directionality on its source. Alex dismissed it as being the usual scent of politicians. I wasn't so certain. The only bright side of being the target of a Mayor Hoynes character assassination would be that everyone who hated him (i.e.: every cop in the city) would buy me drinks until the press died down or until Hoynes found a new target.

So my Captain and LT had a lot to think about.

"Let's have a conversation about who just tried to assassinate you," my LT said, taking the lead. "The patrol guys outside already ran the SWAT truck and the IDs inside. The team lying dead on your stairs are out of the Bronx. They've had a high casualty count, but then, they're SWAT, so that's expected."

I frowned. "The *Bronx*? I'm happy I can even *find* the Bronx. I'm just as happy to forget that the Bronx even exists. If I want to go to the mainland, I go through Staten Island."

Everyone smiled, except for the Captain.

"What's the joke?" he asked.

I maintained strict control over my face. There was always at least one person who never got the joke. "I mean except for the Bronx, the entire city is on an island."

"...Oh. Right."

Mariel came back from the kitchen with a mug of coffee so large, I could put my fist in it. She slid it in front of Alex. He muttered, "Bless you," and took a healthy drag from it.

I held up my hands to refocus us back on the matter that brought everyone into my living room. "Back to the primary topic: Why try to kill me? I don't even know these people. Better yet, I don't even know any of their friends, relatives, or passing acquaintances."

Alex jabbed in my direction with the mug. "But they know you. You've been in the news a lot. Curran? The Women's Health Corps? The death cult? The Mayor?"

Thankfully, Alex had phrased everything in terms that wouldn't get the three of us thrown into a padded cell. What he really meant was *Curran, that serial kill possessed by a demon,* and *that Moloch-Worshiping cultists who brought home sacrifices from their abortion clinic day jobs* and ... okay, in the case of Mayor Hoynes, everyone knew that the man hated my guts. Hoynes probably hated me even more since I had leaked some especially damaging insults about his constituents that he boasted about to Alex and me... and to our body cameras.

Seriously, for a politician, he wasn't that smart. I wish there were a good reason that he had been elected Mayor, but he was merely a supposed libertarian who ran on the Democrat ticket.

But in response to Alex's questions, I rolled my eyes. "That was months ago. Why didn't they come after me back then? I wasn't exactly in hiding. Hell, I had reporters stalking Mariel and Jeremy for *months*. I'd think a few SWAT guys could come and find me. The shooter at the church this morning? He and his friends could have been random EDPs from the internet who hated my guts. But them *and* a SWAT team?"

Alex frowned, shrugged, and drank deeply from the coffee mug. "Well, I don't have any better idea. How about you, L.T.?"

My Lieutenant held his hands up like he was being threatened with an armed weapon. "Don't look at me."

I took a deep breath and let it out slowly. I'd gotten nearly five hours of sleep, but the adrenaline letdown was getting to me. "We may have to table this for tomorrow. Maybe someone can look into the SWAT team, and maybe we can piece together what their problem was? Preferably before one of their friends on the force takes issue with how they tried to kill me, and I got them first? I think—"

My train of thought was derailed by a phone call. I hesitated for a moment. The ring tone was the "Imperial March" by John Williams —Darth Vader's tune. It was the ringtone for "D," the self-proclaimed "gangster" Daniel David DiLeo. I *knew* he was a criminal, but I'd never seen him *do* anything. So I'd never had to arrest him. And he wasn't evil, I would have smelled it on him. Crime was his business, not "thug life"—his and his associates' business uniforms were black leather jackets, black button-down shirts, button-down collars with the top button undone.

As D himself would put it, "You can't think you're gangster if you can't pull up your damn pants."

There were a few scattered black jeans, and they wore their pants belted around their waists.

The short version was that D was a work acquaintance. Very much like the cartoon with Sam the sheepdog and Ralph the coyote, who punch in and punch out of the sheep meadow at either end of the Warner Brothers cartoon. Only D and I were far more cordial when we were both on the clock.

I had listed D as a confidential informant, so I didn't hesitate long before answering the phone. I held it up and explained to the others at the table, "This is my CI, Mister DiLeo. I presume he knows something... I can't think of another reason for him to call."

Everyone shrugged and nodded.

I picked up. "Hey, D. How are you doing?"

"Don't you *hey* me, Detective. Someone just tried to whack me because of you."

I blinked. I had rarely heard D raise his voice. It was even rarer for D to yell in my general direction. But given what he just said, I understood. "Would you care to elaborate on that?"

"Yeah, I'll happily *elaborate,*" D roared. "I nearly got shot by the damn *gang* squad. The *gang squad.* I am a *white collar* criminal, man. The freaking *gang* unit? Just because I'm black. This is insulting. I should've known you'd be a pain in the ass."

I frowned. "Explain what this has to do with me?"

"Don't you pay attention to what happens in your own station? There's a hit out on you on the Dark Web. It's $10 million for your head. They don't even want you alive. It's dead all the way."

Chapter 5

INFERNAL AFFAIRS

"Statler and Waldorf" were an Internal Affairs duo who were obviously older gentlemen. Their real names were Horowitz and McNally, which sounded like a law firm. Even though they were out of Manhattan, they seemed to be permanently assigned to me, out in Queens. We first met over a death in custody inside the station itself. Every time I drew my gun, they seemed to be there sooner or later.

Thankfully, this was the first time that I had seen them in over three months. Yes, though my last major shootout was over half a year earlier, IA had come down on me pretty hard, dissecting every part of my life. However, before the shootout that closed down the Moloch death cult that had kidnapped my son and tried to kill me, Horowitz and McNally had confided in me that much of the pressure that drove them to come after me had come from the Mayor's office. Considering that a Deputy Mayor was the Voodoo man of the cult, I wasn't all that surprised.

The call from D was at nearly three in the morning. The flare went up, and everyone closed ranks. As I said earlier, it's one thing to rat out a cop. It's another thing to try to kill one. News of the Dark Web bounty seemed to make it to the station house before I did.

Internal Affairs had arrived by five.

By the time they had finished debriefing me, it was six.

They leaned back after going over the footage, my testimony, and my family's testimony.

Horowitz started. He was a bit scruffier than McNally, with gray hair and beard. It looked like a professor with tenure who stopped caring what he looked like when he strolled into work. "The NYPD has nearly 40,000 cops who are on the job. Assuming we *only* have a rate of 1% corruption, that's still four hundred crooked cops who would be at least seriously tempted by this cash."

McNally nodded with a frown. "Keep in mind, this is low-balling it. If we had a 1% corruption rate, we'd be bored out of our minds a lot more often than we already are. And we're bored quite a lot. Last time we were bored, we dug into just how many cops fixed parking tickets for their friends and family. Which was about the least shocking thing in the world. Oh, look, every cop has a friend or family member who ended up on the wrong side of the latest arbitrary and capricious ticketing offense the Mayor decides he wants enforced this week. Not a shock. But we're talking about *serious* corruption."

Horowitz conceded the fact. "Let's go big. "Let's say we have a 10% corruption rate."

McNally: "That's 4,000 corrupt cops."

Horowitz: "But that includes all sorts of corruption—"

McNally: "Everything from ticket fixing to bribes to moonlighting as mob button men—"

Horowitz: "So let's say that ten percent of *them* are corrupt enough to want to kill you."

McNally: "That's still four hundred guys."

I frowned. This would not be fun.

Horowitz: "Split the difference and half the first number. That we have a 5% corruption rate—"

McNally: "Which is a lower corruption rate than public school teachers, by the way."

Horowitz: "That still leaves two hundred cops who are willing to kill a fellow police officer for the right price."

McNally: "Which is an awful lot of guns, bombs and cop cars out to kill you and anyone in the way."

I held up my hands. Their back-and-forth -dialogue was giving me a headache. I hadn't expected them to keep going. "Hold on a second. Let's figure this out logically, okay? Because I think the reasonable first step is to figure out who hates me enough to want me dead, and who can *afford* a bounty this big. Because, honestly, while I have stepped on more than a few toes in my time, I can't imagine who has that much loose change floating around out there."

Horowitz and McNally exchanged a look. I followed the exchange of glances and tried to interpret them. When that failed, I simply asked, "What? What is it?"

Horowitz looked sheepish. He shrugged. "Well, you see..."

McNally: "Remember Rene Ormeno?"

I felt the bottom of my stomach fall out. Rene Ormeno had been a distraction during my ordeal with Christopher Curran, the serial killer who had been possessed by the demon. He was a senior officer in MS-13, which was one part mafia and one part terrorist organization. Their relentless violence was all to further their moneymaking schemes—human trafficking, sex slavery, guns, and drugs.

The last time I saw Ormeno, he had his own private padded cell in the loony bin. He had to be strapped to the wall every waking hour. Before I had taken down the possessed murderer at Rikers Island, the legion within him had possessed a large chunk of the prison population – including Ormeno. When the demons had been banished, Ormeno had been reduced to a raving, gibbering maniac...except when I entered his cell. Then he was stone cold sane. Apparently, I had that effect.

I could still see his crazy eyes when he snapped from being a rambling lunatic to a creature with agency-- evil agency that willed nothing more than to destroy me.

But thinking of Ormeno as being anywhere else but in that cell made the world go sideways. "What *about* Ormeno?"

"Well, ya see—" Horowitz started

"Ormeno is out." McNally finished

"Yeah. He's free," Horowitz concluded

I blinked. I felt like I had been gut punched. "What do you mean that he's free? Last time I saw him, he was a total nutcase. A danger to himself *and* to others."

McNally shrugged. "He got better."

My jaw dropped. "That's impossible considering ..."

Considering what, Tommy? I thought. *Considering that a demon had left its mark in Ormeno's brain? Considering that your presence was the only thing that seemed to calm the—heh—demons in his head? Go ahead, smart guy, say something.*

"Considering the last time I saw him," I said weakly.

Horowitz shrugged this time. "Don't ask us, Detective Nolan. We're not shrinks."

"However, he is a clue," McNally added

"Because gee, I wonder if MS-13 could raise ten million," speculated Horowitz.

I frowned, my brows furrowing. "Wait a second. If he 'got better', I thought that the DEA and ICE *also* wanted Ormeno? They wanted him to flip on Thirteen? Right?"

They exchanged another glance. They had an entire conversation pass between them that I couldn't hear. It was starting to get on my nerves.

McNally: "It's in part a combination of lawyers, judges, ACLU reps, his time in the rubber room, and he's been out of circulation for nearly a year."

Horowitz: "Who knows if the DEA even wants him anymore?"

McNally: "MS-13's entire operation could have changed."

Horowitz: "Which means that Ormeno is useless."

McNally: "Besides, welcome to NYC's asylum policy. Both illegal and mental"

Horowitz: "It's difficult even deporting illegals who are high-profile murderers."

My brain was starting to hurt. "But Ormeno is a monster."

McNally: "And?"

Horowitz: "... so, Tommy, have you ever considered WitSec?"

I stared at them both for a long moment, saying nothing. After all, it was a lot to take in, and their blitz style of conversation was faster than Wimbledon.

Go on the run. It was unthinkable. Imagine, being part of a police force with a paramilitary wing, its own foreign intelligence service, a small army that could go toe-to-toe with the National Guard for a few rounds ... and then being told to run and hide because *maybe* a few dozen of them were bad actors.

But then, Mariel and Jeremy and our unborn child. They were just as much at risk. How would they react under continuous threat? I knew that living with me came with its own problems. Heck, living with me was constantly being in condition red. Had we gone another month with peace and quiet on the home front, we might have even relaxed enough to be taken by surprise. What if Mariel and Jeremy had been caught in a crossfire? What if the SWAT team had used an RPG or threw a grenade through my window? What would have happened if we hadn't been ready for them? Would the SWAT team have murdered my entire family as well? I couldn't imagine a situation where they could have acted otherwise—the situation would have compelled them to assassinate all of us. Staying outside of police protection? That was akin to suicide.

... Though, on the other hand, I had been awakened by an angel of the Lord. The timing was too suspicious to have been otherwise. I had been instructed to smite the agents of Satan. Somehow, I couldn't imagine that a handful of corrupt cops knocking down my front door was the extent of the command. I had literally been handed an order from God. How the department shrinks would love me: "auditory hallucinations" would probably buy me a full pension disability.

I immediately sobered. *Tell me this isn't my ego running amok. "On a mission from God"? Does this even sound like me? Or did I finally just drive off the deep end of what I think I'm capable of, with or without God's help? Because, Lord, no offense, while I am certain that with You all things are possible ... are You going to make me bulletproof? Or, more importantly, my family? Have gale-force winds hurl grenades sideways? You're all powerful, but if I'm your pointman on this, then I'm going to need a lot of divine intervention...more than usual, I mean.*

Sigh. Here I am Lord. Bring it.

I said aloud, "I'm a cop. We don't run."

A split second later, the RPG hit the front door.

Chapter 6

DOING THE STATIONS

The rocket-propelled grenade slammed into the arch of the front door. All security glass was reduced to glitter. The door frame was ripped from the concrete, hurling it into the station. The two officers in front were instantly killed. One had been decapitated by the RPG as it shot past. The other one was blown in half.

Inside the station, the shock wave ripped through the front desk, the waiting area, and the bullpen. The glass dividers that separated the officers were blasted out. The relatively new vending machine went flying and crashed through a wall.

Half a dozen cops were killed instantly. None of the two dozen civilians in the front lobby, waiting for everything as varied as parking tickets and copies of police reports, to waiting for their lawyer, survived the first explosion.

The white panel van across the street didn't hesitate. Both side doors had been opened for the RPG to fire without turning the inside of the van into a crematorium. The one who fired the RPG tossed it aside and picked up a machine gun as the driver backed up half a block, put it in gear, then charged for the front door. They tried to plow through the line of cop cars parked on the sidewalk at right angles to the precinct. One of the cars was the one that Alex and I used on a daily basis. The impact with the white panel van caused our car to explode. It blew the white van back, off of its front wheels, and onto the roof, like a turtle flipped onto its shell.

However, that explosion was powerful enough to create a wide gap in the line of cars. That was good enough for the next car to speed in, charging for the gap in the front door. It sped in, smashing though what was left of the front desk, and through a divider separating the bull pen from the offices.

The gunman burst out of the car, spraying the surrounding area with bullets, even though everyone who was still alive was on the floor, and they were shooting at hip-height.

The gunmen were dressed in "street gang casual," in leather jackets… even though it was the middle of July … in wife beater T-shirts, and some wore no shirts at all. All of them, however, were covered in tattoos, from their scalps to the ankles. Which was standard for lifelong members of MS-13.

Meanwhile, I was upstairs with Statler, Waldorf, and Alex. The explosion rocked the building, and we were all thrown from our chairs. We weren't going to get any paperwork done today.

I pushed to my feet and rushed for the door. "Come on."

I was running down the hall, past Alex. He was already on his feet, gun drawn. My Browning Hi-Powered was already in the evidence locker. Thankfully, I still had my 9mm service weapon.

Then I heard the automatic fire and considered that I might need a bigger gun.

I charged downstairs anyway. The automatic fire was still on the first floor. Other cops went behind me, into the basement, where we kept the armory. No one was dumb enough to try to engage automatic weapons just in uniform. Even the Kevlar vests we're given aren't enough to take that type of punishment.

Then I noticed that the MS-13 shooters were firing from the hip, barely looking where they fired. The three on my side of the car had their back to the three on the other side of the car, and vice versa. They were firing on full automatic, partially to keep everyone's head down. The few cops left on the first floor were firing as much as they could.

In short, they weren't looking. They were also functionally deaf. They relied on the chaos to keep everyone off balance.

I slipped through the partially open door, walking low and fast. I moved along the back of the wall, using desks to break line of sight. I stopped in front of the car's bumper. I was to the left side of the shooters on the passenger side of the car. I was to the side of all of them.

I popped up just enough to aim. I took aim at the driver's side shooters, since fewer cops were giving them trouble on that side.

I opened fire.

The first bullet hit the driver in the ear. His head snapped to one side, throwing him into the gunman next to him. The second gunman cursed and spun, knocking his fallen comrade off of him. He was still angry when I fired three more times in a Mozambique drill —two bullets to the chest, one to the head. He fell right back into the third gunman on the driver's side. I didn't even have the chance to open fire on the last one, since he was caught by one of the cops he'd been shooting at.

I redirected my fire to the passenger side ... just in time for the nearest one to turn and see me.

Oh darn.

I fired reflexively, without aiming.

The bullet caught the AK-47 in the muzzle. I don't mean it struck the barrel, or the sight. It struck the muzzle, corking the opening. It was a 9mm being slamming into a 7.62 mm opening with the force of a few thousand feet per second. It jammed in the barrel through the force of the pressure.

The gunman fired.

If you've ever seen what happens when a cartoon character jams a finger into a pistol, the effects were similar. The explosion ruined his hands, split the barrel, and smashed gun shrapnel into his lower body like a fragmentation grenade.

I frowned. *Thank you, God.*

The next two gunmen turned as their partner fell. It was enough of a distraction for the remaining cops to gun them down.

I knew we weren't out of the woods just yet. There were still gunmen outside who were probably on their way inside. I holstered my pistol and ran forward. The car wasn't locked, so I swung in and popped the trunk.

In the trunk was what I was looking for: guns. Lots of guns. Including several grenades.

I looked around. Packard came out the stairwell door. I pondered a moment what had taken him so long. I hadn't realized that it had only been seconds since I came out of the stairwell myself.

"Alex!" I called. "You used to play baseball, right?"

"Yeah?"

I raised one of the grenades. "How's your fastball?"

The MS-13 troops closed in on the front entrance. The first wave had a six-man formation.

The first man to die was the third man in the formation. He died not from a gunshot, or an explosion, but from a grenade, fast-balled into his face. The metal pineapple killed him on impact.

His buddy kept his eyes on the goal, straight ahead. He stepped around his fallen comrade. In all of the commotion and gunfire, he didn't realize what had felled his buddy.

None of them knew what killed them.

With the nearest gunmen cleared, the remaining cops and I moved to what was left of the entrance, spraying cover fire for Alex. He threw the next three grenades in rapid succession, clearing out the gunman to the left and the right flanks of our attackers. The resulting explosions caused even more panic. They also drove the gunmen to the center of their line of attack, clumping together...

Making them an easier target.

Alex threw four grenades this time, one right after the other. We were bowling for gangstas, and Alex threw a perfect game.

Alex tossed two more grenades than needed. All it did was make new potholes in the street. But it was Queens, who would notice?

An explosion then ripped through the back door. I whipped

around. The frontal attack was a diversion. I dashed forward, stepping on the trunk of the car in the middle of the bullpen. I jumped onto the roof, then the hood, and ran to the back hallway.

I slammed into the gunmen coming out of the back hallway. We all went down in a pile of limbs and ammo. At point-blank range, I fired randomly, one bullet per attacker, and circled back, firing again. I emptied the magazine, then started swatting them with the empty gun.

After a minute of thrashing around, Alex grabbed me by the shoulder and pulled me off the pile of gunmen. "Down, butch. I think you got them."

I blinked. I had taken them all out of the fight.

I slumped.

"This gets better and better," I gasped.

A rack of a shotgun filled the eerie post-battle silence.

Alex and I looked over our shoulders. Sergeant Mary Russell stood behind us, shotgun pointed directly at us. She racked it and took aim.

"Sorry, guys," she said softly. "I have bills to pay."

I grabbed Alex and swung him around, hoping to shield him with my body. If I absorbed enough pellets, Alex could open fire and drop her before she could kill him. I slammed Alex against the wall and slammed my own side right next to him, creating as tight a seal as possible so he wouldn't even be scratched.

Two blasts went off at the same time, turning into one large *boom*.

I hesitated for a moment. I felt nothing.

I moved away from the wall, turning around to where Russell had been a moment before. Instead of the Sergeant, there was McNally and Horowitz, guns drawn. The two older men had revolvers.

Mary Russell, who I had considered my friend, was dead on the floor.

The IA guys lowered their guns and sighed.

McNally shook his head. "We haven't had to pull our guns in—"

"Decades," Horowitz concluded. "The bad old days."

I winced. How long had these two been on the force? There's old (for a cop), and then there's *old*.

McNally holstered his weapon. His wrist beeped, and he looked at his wristwatch/heart monitor. "Damn it. My heart rate is up. My doctor is going to kill me."

Chapter 7

ON THE DL

I spent the better part of the rest of the day after the shoot-out walking the scene. I was uncertain of how the MS-13 attack failed. Yes, we managed to intercept the pointmen in the lobby. Yes, we stole enough of their grenades to orbit the owners of Planet Hollywood. But they opened with an RPG attack that could have wiped us out if they had kept it up.

Within the first fifteen minutes, I kept coming back to the opening of the attack from the white van. It had been blown onto its roof. There was a giant crater in the middle of the sidewalk, where my car had been when this all started. It shouldn't have really stood out in the middle of the all the other holes, but this one was more obvious, and bigger. Fragmentation grenades weren't meant to blast through concrete like this.

There had been a bomb in our car.

I groaned. *Lovely. Bombers, too. I wonder if they're bomb squad, or if there's someone else who could have slipped past.*

"What's the matter?" Alex said behind me.

I pointed out the crater and the white van and explained.

He rolled his eyes. "Great. Time to put you in WitSec. Now."

I shook my head. "Can't do that."

Alex sighed. "Sure. Of course you can't. Can we at least get Mariel and Jeremy off to a safe house."

I arched my brow. "Where do you think we could go that would guarantee that no cops would be tempted by ten million dollars? Mary just tried to kill us. *Mary.* Who has been at the desk for how long? I can't even remember."

Alex frowned. "So we don't use cops? Maybe feds?" He grimaced. "Yeah, because feds don't have bills to pay either. Never mind."

"You see my problem."

"Hey! I thought I was the cynical one."

I chuckled. "This is my moment to be as clever as a serpent. Innocent as a dove can come later."

I had three ideas about what to do with my family. Technically, there were only two of them. I had friends in the Catholic Church, and there were two places within the Church I could think about. One place would be with my friend Father Freeman. But he was also a police psychologist, degrees and everything. That made him far too close for comfort. Not that I thought he was a threat, but he had too many cops too close to him. Hiding Mariel and Jeremy with him wouldn't guarantee their safety. I had personal connections with the Church as well, which was a problem.

I had one more option, short of taking my family outside of the tri-state area, which also wasn't a bad idea.

I slid out my cell phone and found the number I needed.

"What do you want, Detective?" D answered. He still sounded a little snarly from earlier this morning.

"Have you moved your family to a safe house?" I asked him. "Because I'd like to add one or two more people to the bunker."

MY FAMILY HAD ONLY one rifle, a shotgun, and two handguns between Jeremy and Mariel. I still had my weapons. Statler and Waldorf didn't take my two on-duty weapons, which surprised me. But then again, they were in the action, so they weren't even in charge of investigating the shootout.

Either way, I told the two of them that my family was going off the grid for a while. The IA team thought that I was going to join them in hiding. It was a temptation, to be honest. But as I told Statler and Waldorf, I couldn't run and hide. I didn't know if this was building to a head, or if this was only a buildup to something worse.

Ugh. Something worse. What could be worse than a demon serial killer and a death cult, with their own Bokor and a few zombies to boot?

The first thing to come to mind was the warlock. I didn't have something else to latch on to. When Rene Ormeno of MS-13 was in the nuthouse, he had waxed psychotic about a warlock who was out to get me...but, obviously, the warlock hadn't confronted me yet, because I was still alive at the time. Ormeno had been nuts ... except when I was in the room. Then, he was crystal clear that I was going to get killed.

Hopefully, this isn't the time for fighting the warlock. Otherwise, I might just get killed in the crossfire.

I brought my family to an apartment complex about twenty stories tall. It was located in a nice area called Bayside. It was an interesting place to meet D and his "bunker," since Bayside was a primarily Jewish neighborhood, and oh boy, did D not look Jewish.

Today, we were met by one of the security officers for the apartment complex. She was a pleasant-looking brunette in an Allied Universal uniform. She met us and took the three of us up to an apartment—Alex stayed in the car.

The apartment was on a lower floor. Thinking tactically, I could only conclude that D wanted to smash out the windows and lower themselves to street level.

Despite wanting to take the stairs, we took the elevator (call me paranoid, but being locked in a suspended metal box with people out to kill me didn't seem like a great idea). The guard had bad knees, and Mariel gave me a look when I suggested taking several guns and hundreds of rounds of ammo up a flight of stairs.

The guard took us to the apartment at the end of the hall, nearest the stairs.

The door opened. D stood in the doorway, filling it. Today he wore a navy-blue suit, and a gold tie with the Vatican keys all over it. Daniel David DiLeo and I had more or less come up together. I had been on the streets as a uniform while he had been running numbers. This was after D had graduated from child bike-courier. He basically went from bike messenger to MBA in ten easy years. I didn't ask too many details about what he may have done during his less savory years. I had always known that he was the best of a lot of bad options. He ran multiple legitimate operations. To my knowledge, he hadn't sold drugs in years. He owned guns, but didn't sell any, as far as I knew.

And the only people I'm certain that D had killed had all been in my defense. If there was anyone outside of my family or my partner that I could trust, it was D. The last thing he would do is try to collect on the bounty. He would especially avoid collecting the bounty in his own safe house.

"Come in, quickly."

We did, then I made introductions. D had a nice little apartment. The door opened to an open living room. To the right was the kitchen, sealed off from the rest of the living room. As we walked in, I could see that the corner of the living room (going around the kitchen) was a small offshoot with a dining room table. The boundary of the room was a couch, facing a giant, wall-mounted television. There were no blank spaces of wall. Bookcases lined the apartment.

"Lovely home," Mariel said. "Thank you for letting us in."

He shrugged. "Don't thank me yet. We're going to need to talk about one or two things."

Before D could say more, a stunning young woman walked in from the hallway branching off the living room. She was tall and leggy, with a black and white skirt that fell below her knees. Her hair was long and straight. Her nails were perfectly manicured with white

French tips on them. Her posture was model-perfect and elegant. She was black, with dark hair and eyes to match.

"Hello," she said in a smooth, rich voice. "I'm Anna. You must be Detective Nolan."

I nodded as I shook her hand. "Correct. This is my wife Mariel, and my son Jeremy."

D stepped closer and wrapped an arm around her tiny frame. "Anna is my wife."

I blinked. I knew that D had a daughter named Julie he loved intensely. He was faithful to his many girlfriends. While he wasn't the type to refer to a woman as a "baby momma," this was the first time I had heard of a wife.

D smiled. "Don't worry, Detective. I don't advertise. It's bad for business."

I nodded slowly, noting that his elocution was even better than normal, and he usually spoke better than I did. Occasionally, I had heard him pronounce it "bidness." But at that moment, I wondered how many of the "slips" in elocution were deliberate attempts to throw me off. I knew better than to ask for an explanation.

Jeremy, however, didn't. "Why not?"

D looked down at my son and smiled. "Because there are people I deal with who think that being committed to one person is not cool and that working a full-time job is 'acting white.' So it's for her protection."

Jeremy cocked his head. "Are you a superhero, too, like Daddy?"

D shook his head gently. Jeremy didn't casually refer to me as a superhero that often. "Not quite like your father, no. Though you could say this is my secret identity." He looked to me. "We must talk."

I followed D into an office just off of that hall. I closed the door behind me. "We come with our own artillery if we need it."

"That's not what I'm concerned about. Have a seat." D sat in an office chair built for his bulk. I sat on the ottoman against the wall. "Why me?" he asked.

I nodded. Bringing my family to D was unusual. "Even my fellow police officers are tempted by ten million dollars. Someone I considered at least a good work acquaintance, maybe even a friend, tried to kill me this morning. Anyone I could think of within the state has ties to the cops, or close ties to me."

"You're tied to me," D rumbled. "You insist on filing me in your DD5s."

I shrugged. "Yes, but you're better armed than the Catholic Church."

D chuckled at that. "Point taken."

I nodded towards the living room. "So. Anna?"

D grinned. "It's like I said, man. Public displays of matrimony are a great way to get folks killed."

I shrugged. "And here I thought that your 'image as self-defense' stopped at your public displays of being 'gangsta.'"

D rolled his eyes and readjusted his bulk. "Please. These numbnuts who keep their pants pulled down think they're cool, except what they're doing is a jail sign saying that they're available for a hook up behind bars. They're idiots, man. But they think someone is all 'resspecable,' " he said with air quotes and deliberately slurred speech, "they believe that he's a soft target. I could spend weeks or months fighting off enough bozos to prove to them, once more, that no, I'm not soft. But that would require more effort than I want to expend, hitting fools who come at me. Though as you've seen, I have weapons in case I need to do that."

I laughed that time. D had been part of my backup during the assault on the death cult. He had gone up against real gunmen, as well as zombie gunmen, and probably would have taken out the Bokor if D hadn't been knocked out. And since the Bokor had unnatural strength, it said something that D wasn't dead.

"Pity you can't take credit for the hit out at King's Point."

D shrugged. He frowned a moment, considering his next statement. "So, we never did talk about all the zombies. What *was* up with that?"

I paused for a long moment there. On the one hand, King's Point was merely a nice neighborhood. On the other hand, it was also the final stand of the WHC a few months ago. "It's hard to explain."

"That much I figured. Make it easy."

"Remember Christopher Curran? The serial killer?" D nodded, and I continued. "He was possessed by a demon."

D hesitated a moment. His thoughts played out all over his face, from incredulous furrowed brow to "No, that makes sense" bunched lips and back again. "That makes sense of certain things. What did that have to do with King's Point?"

"They raised the demon."

D sighed. "Of course, they did." His expression then changed. His eyes squinted with amusement. "Now, what about *you*?"

This was the moment I dreaded. When the supernatural came up before, so did my little secret relationship with God. Or maybe I should say His relationship with me. "What about me?"

D smiled. "Nate Brindle got out of Rikers. I'm told you're a Jedi now?"

The bottom fell out of my stomach. During the demon's incarceration, he had started a riot in jail at Rikers Island. Though I should be more specific ... the *legion of demons* within the serial killer Curran had run rampant, starting a riot. Inmate Nate Brindle had been instrumental in helping me quell parts of the riot. He'd also seen me die and fade away. I hadn't explained that I could bi-locate (in that instant, it was tri-locate) and Brindle had concluded I must have been a Jedi. I hadn't corrected him.

"I pray a lot," I answered. "And God listens. In my case, He says *yes* more than He says no. I suspect a lot of it has to do with me being up against supernatural forces of darkness. Therefore, God grants me ways around it."

D's only reaction was for his eyebrows to twitch up a little. "You're saying you have superpowers now?"

I sighed. No matter how many times I had to do it, I was always wary and uncomfortable trying to explain this to other people. "I'm saying I have superpowers when I need them. I don't exactly use them so I can casually take a day off and come into work at the same time."

"Uh huh."

I opened my mouth to say more when I was struck with a horrible smell. It was something I hadn't been hit with in months. It was the stench of evil. It was foul and overpowering. I had only smelled it around the truly vile: the demon, the death cult, and Rene Ormeno.

I was up from the chair in a shot. I said "On me" to D as I opened the door and dashed down the hall. I drew my handgun as I entered the living room. I spun towards the door, gun up, as the door came crashing in. I fired at a distance of ten feet. I couldn't miss.

The first two through the door were shambling zombies. They showed obvious signs of decay. But they were stable enough to hold machetes. Instead of a Mozambique drill, I fired three to the face of the first one, then dropped to a crouch and blasted away both knees. The first zombie fell to the floor, still squirming, but harmless. I readjusted my aim for the next zombie, but a loud blast from behind me struck it in the shoulder. Its shoulder exploded, and the zombie fell back. I added two rounds under the chin for good measure.

Four people wheeled around the door frame in the hall. Two were down in a crouch and two more were standing. All of them armed. All of their pointed their guns straight at me.

I fired, and the world exploded around me.

Chapter 8

BLUE MOUNTAIN

The gunfire rocked me. I had caught one of the attackers as his gun leveled at my face. The bullet caught him squarely in the bridge of his nose and dropped him. He had been the one in a crouch, at the right side of the door frame.

However, at least one of the next three guns had a solid lock on me.

Almost the same second I fired, the shotgun behind me went off again. It caught the crouched gunman on the other side.

The explosion directly behind me, over my head, seriously rang my bell. Both of the remaining two gunman fell.

I didn't look at who shot who, but I darted forward to the door. I remained in a crouch as I looked around the doorway. There were both more zombies and more living attackers in the hallway.

I ducked back into the apartment. "Honey. Rifle."

D laughed so loud, I even heard it over the ringing in my ears. I looked up, and he dual-wielded 50-cal Desert Eagles. That's how he'd taken down two at once. Mariel had the shotgun behind him.

"First," D said, "don't call me honey. And don't worry, Detective. You're in my house. Also, all of the apartments on this floor are filled with my guys."

Gunshots came from the hallway. I waited for a moment, then looked out. The floor was carpeted with fresh bodies ... and less fresh zombies.

"See, told you," D said. "It's how we keep the apartment. No witnesses live on this floor, just my men."

I nodded. It was the only thing I could do. I was going to ask how D managed to remain hidden in a heavily Jewish neighborhood when he clearly wasn't. But if all of his immediate neighbors were his men, really, who'd notice? If he really wanted to be a secret, he'd simply not go out through the front door, but through some other level—the basement, the garage, the kitchen if he so chose.

"And the upper floors won't hear the gunshots?"

"I have an agreement with security. The neighbors will call building security. They and I will talk. No big deal. The real problem, though, is how they found us. No one knows about this place. And we're real careful about going in and out of here."

I nodded. I shared his concern. I went for the nearest gunman's body and turned him over. The gunman was black, with long dread-locks that went halfway down his back.

"Jamaicans," D muttered. "I hate these guys. They can be annoying."

I frowned. "I guess that explains the zombies."

"The word on the Dark Web is spreading, apparently."

I bent down and frisked the four gunmen. On the fourth, I found a map of New York City and a crystal on a rope.

From the couch, D's wife Anna asked, "Am I hallucinating, or is that a scrying crystal?"

I nodded. I had seen something like this on the History Channel. One of Hitler's occultist buddies had scried for a sunken warship and found it. What they used had been something like this.

It was also pointed out that when scrying for a *person*, it helped to have clothing, a bit of hair, nails, or something else that once belonged to the person targeted. I didn't want to think of how many different things could have been used. Hell, someone could have gone through my old house and took hair out of the drains. Then again, given that fellow cops were coming after me, checking my locker after this was all over wasn't that bad an idea.

"This isn't the same guy?" D asked. "He sounded more Haitian before you whacked him. But how many people can do zombies?"

I frowned thoughtfully. I didn't have the heart to tell D that, even though we had thrown the creature that called itself Bokor Baracus into a massive fire pit meant for burning sacrifices to Moloch, he was still alive. Apparently, he was also the "Deputy Mayor for Social Justice" or some other stupid made-up name. I didn't know if we had faced down a double, like a golem made of flesh, or a homunculus, or what. Maybe he was also able to bi-locate. Ever since I ran into the demon, I decided to research everything I could about my condition and my abilities. However, when you type "bi-location" into Wikipedia, the page for it notes that it was also a trick that the occultist Aleister Crowley also claimed to have. If it were truly something the dark side could pull off, this would get complicated.

Well, more complicated than it had been already.

"If they can find you, does that mean we need to lock down the building?" D asked.

I shook my head and stood. "No. I had no beef with these guys before today. I didn't know they existed, and probably the reverse is also true. They had to scry to get my location. If they did that, then they wouldn't have shared that information. No one wants to share a bounty, even if it is ten million dollars. If they were willing to share, they would have had more gunmen, fewer zombies. Anyone else wants to find me again, they'll have to do a fresh scry, and I'm going to be out of here."

"Point taken. Walk with me."

This time, we took the stairs. D holstered his guns before we started down.

"First, where are you and Alex going to go?"

"Ormeno is out of jail."

D paused on a step but caught up. "Any reason why?"

"We're an asylum city, remember? Apparently, flouting federal law is *in*."

D shook his head. "I never thought I'd hear myself worried about the cops *not* enforcing the law. Do you have any ideas where he might be?"

"Not a clue. I'm going to have to do some checking. Unless you have any feelers out on MS-13."

"Since Ormeno was arrested, they've been more interested in getting him out than trying to expand. I guess they felt he was really just that important. He's as good a place to start as any."

I nodded, adding nothing else. But the thought process was easy. If one made a Venn diagram about the people who hated me to levels of homicidal intent and overlapped it with people who could afford ten million dollars, there weren't many... technically.

Sure, Rene Ormeno wasn't personally wealthy. But if he could direct the entire wealth of MS-13 against me, then yes, $10 million wouldn't be a stretch.

On the other hand, the Mayor—or his deputy—could easily raise that sort of cash.

If there were any hidden assets from the cult or the Women's Health Corps, then any random cultist with access could come at me ...

So, that really meant there's any number of random Cultists or MS-13 members who might want my head.

So at the end of the day, there was only one thing that made sense: investigate the people we know. That meant Ormeno, Deputy Mayor Baracus, and maybe Mayor Hoynes himself. Perhaps one of the latter two was this "Warlock" that Ormeno had talked about in the loony bin.

Either way, we were going to find the source of this menace, and we were going to put a stake through its black heart. Literally or metaphorically, whichever worked best.

"Are you going to be working alone?"

I shook my head. "Alex is in the car."

"Ah, yes, the esteemed Detective Packard."

"I'm sure he'll be thrilled to hear you refer to him as that."

"Indeed." We got to the bottom of the stairs, and he opened the door leading outside for me. "You'll have to walk out the rest of the way. Sorry about not seeing you to your car, but I would like to keep a low profile."

"Understandable."

"That being said, don't be surprised if Packard is a little putout. I had my men bring you a gift."

I frowned, slightly worried about what gift that could be. D laughed. "Don't worry. It's nothing *that* interesting."

I shrugged, thanked him again, and he just waved me away.

When I arrived back at the car, Alex stood by the driver's side and gave me a look like I had been away forever. "What took you?"

"Didn't you hear the gunshots?"

"Yeah. I was expecting an Armada of cops to come up at any time, but no one did. What the Hell?"

"Long story, get in, and I'll tell you."

"No, first thing's first. I have to tell you about the new toys."

Alex reached down and pulled the trunk switch. It popped open. I walked around.

The trunk was now heavy with guns and ammo. It looked like the SHOT gun showroom. There were two MP5 submachine guns, two M4 automatic rifles, and boxes upon boxes of ammo. In the back of the trunk was even a box or two of grenades...stacked atop boxes of ammo. Included was a Thompson submachine gun and two barrels of ammunition.

"Huh. Well, that's interesting." I closed the trunk.

Alex smiled. "I particularly like that he gave you a Tommy gun."

I rolled my eyes. "Yes. I get it. Considering what just happened, I don't blame him for the caution ... I do blame him for the bad joke."

As we pulled out, I explained about the Jamaicans trying to kill us, and how they came prepared with zombies.

"Zombies?" Packed yelled. He cursed. "I thought this supernatural crap was because of demons and death cults and shit. Now you're telling me that almost anyone can use this hocus pocus insanity?"

I shrugged as I made a turn. "What do you want? For the

Kingdom of Heaven, many are called, but few are chosen. Hell, however, is open to everyone. There are pearly gates for a reason."

"Lovely. Hell has an open borders policy. Can't they build a wall like everyone else?"

"Give it time."

"So, where are we heading now?"

"MS-13."

Alex said nothing for a moment. I stopped at a sign and looked at him. He wasn't even surprised. I moved forward again. After a moment, he said, "Well, that tells me who, but not where."

I laughed. "Where do you figure?"

It didn't take him more than a couple of beats. "Ah. Gotcha. So, Harlem or Long Island."

While "Harlem" is generally considered a black neighborhood, that isn't the extent of it. Technically, that Harlem is *West* Harlem. That area has had a renaissance, the Apollo Theater, and several strong cultural movements that more or less ended when the Black Panthers came to town. (For the record, the Black Panther political movement came several months *after* the superhero of the same name. The Marvel character debuted in July 1966, while the Black Panther Party was created that October. In 1969, they were in New York and trying to blow up buildings).

East Harlem, on the other hand, is Spanish Harlem, simply referred to as "The Barrio." Even that may not be true in a few years, as the Chinese had started to move there in droves.

East Harlem is north of the Upper East Side and East 96th Street, up to about East 142nd Street, east of Fifth Avenue to the water. Some people don't consider it part of Harlem at all—at which point, someone should tell the labels on the buses that read "East Harlem." As you can tell from its name, neighborhood is predominantly Latino. It's probably the largest Latino community New York City. Its majority is Puerto Rican, with a large minority of Dominicans, Cubans and Mexican immigrants—legal or not. It absorbed what had once been *Italian* Harlem.

So if you're a tourist in New York, don't *just* ask for "Harlem." You may get lost.

Another difference between West and East Harlem—as I said, while West Harlem had had the Harlem Renaissance, the Barrio never fared as well. It was plagued with the highest jobless rate in the city, teenage pregnancy, AIDS, drug abuse, homelessness, and an asthma rate five times the national average. Add to that the second-highest concentration of public housing in the United States.

"How about Long Island? If MS-13 were in the Barrio, the Latin Kings would object. I haven't heard of any shootouts or assassinations lately."

Meanwhile, out on Long Island, there were estimates between one and two thousand thugs. They were out in some of the less savory areas in central Suffolk: Hempstead Station, Central Islip, and the notorious Brentwood. The latter held the most interest for us. Despite the insults hurled at it, Brentwood wasn't really a slum. It was a range of upper to lower class. It was less about economics in the area, and more about how bad the bad areas really were.

Due to the geographical and political oddities of New York, Brentwood wasn't a city. Brentwood is technically a "hamlet" in the Town of Islip in the county of Suffolk.

Confused yet? So are most of the occupants.

Way back in the middle of the 19th century, Brentwood was merely a stop on the Long Island Rail Road as it expanded into the heart of the island. Within the decade, it became a "Utopian community" named Modern Times. A decade after *that,* it was renamed Brentwood after the town in Essex, England.

Nowadays, it is the home of Pilgrim Psychiatric Center. Fifty-two acres of the psychiatric center was converted into the Brentwood State Park athletic field complex. That is more or less its own joke about insanity and state-backed anything.

If anyone ever tells you that Long Island is some sort of mythical Whites Only area, smack them. While there was a mix of ethnicity all over the Island, Brentwood alone had a 70% Latino population. They even had a consulate for El Salvador.

Brentwood was only ten square miles and home to 60,664. Making it not only a good place for a few hundred MS-13 members to live in, but the economic diversity also gave them targets to rob and people to sell to—be it drugs, prostitutes, or sex slaves.

If Rene Ormeno was going for the "needle in a haystack" method of hiding, Brentwood was one of the easier places to hide.

Alex finally said, "I presume you're figuring that, out of our possible suspects, Ormeno's the best?"

I nodded. "Maybe. But he's the easiest to identify, since we know him, and easiest to get to since both the mayor and his deputy should be protected by a ring of bodyguards."

"Yeah. For guys who are against gun ownership, they do seem to be surrounded by them."

I concurred. I continued, giving Alex the same rationale that I had given D.

"I don't disagree. And frankly, I think that the best outcome is that Ormeno is the one who's after you. Because if the deputy mayor is after you, I can't imagine how we can touch the guy short of going completely rogue."

I gave him a brief look as I made my way to the Cross Island Expressway. "You mean we're not already?"

"We're not completely rogue if the bosses haven't suspended us."

I was about to tell him that he'd seen too many movies when I felt a strong compulsion to turn on the police radio. Don't even question why. I felt the need so badly, my hand moved almost of its own accord. I went to the wide band scanner.

The car radio blurted immediately, "Repeat, there is a 187 at," and rattled off a street address. "Code Purple. Again, 187, Code purple at," and the address again.

My foot pressed down on the pedal, and I sped for the exit for the Grand Central Parkway. "Get the bubble gum machine, Alex."

He did as I asked, putting the police light on the roof of the car as I shot down the Cross Island. He didn't even ask what I was doing as I got onto the GCP westbound ramp.

Almost everyone knows that a 187 is a homicide. Less well known is that a "Code Purple" was radio code for gang activity. The address was in East Harlem. So Alex knew what my first thoughts were.

Though I didn't tell him that this was less driven by a gut feeling and more by Divine Guidance. I didn't know if God personally was guiding my hand, but I would take it.

Against you, oh Lord, who can stand? Let's roll.

Chapter 9

INTO DARKNESS

The apartment complex was massive. Insanely huge. A typical block of Manhattan real estate was about 100,000 square feet, or more than two acres.

This was an apartment complex that filled the entire block and then went up twenty stories. It was an ugly brown brick box that would have fit perfectly in the Soviet Union.

The address we had gotten over the radio led us to this apartment. The crime scene was out in front. At least three men were dead on the street. "At least" three because they were in pieces and parts. Given the spatter on the street, they had been thrown out of the apartment building. Since the windows weren't shattered, they must have been thrown from the roof. Given the tattoos on an arm of a body close to the police tape, the three corpses had been members of the Latin Kings.

I pulled up to the crime scene tape and stood outside of it to avoid alerting anyone of my presence. We had even disabled the GPS signal from the police car before leaving the station. It would defeat the purpose to announce ourselves.

Though as soon as I took a deep breath, I knew we were on the right track.

I could smell Rene Ormeno's evil. I couldn't tell if he was still in the area or not, but he'd been there.

I wandered back to the car and stuck my head in. "Alex, you want to stay in the car, or risk the police placard?"

He shrugged. "We park ourselves next to the other cop cars, who'll notice? You're not going in by yourself. And you're sure as Hell not taking one of D's toy guns. Neither of us are wearing coats long enough."

I frowned. I hadn't even considered taking one of D's automatic weapons. The major problem there would be that this apartment complex would be more overcrowded than a bar offering free beer on Fifth Avenue during Saint Patrick's Day. Even using my handguns there worried me.

For those of you out in the gun world who are saying "get frangible rounds!" That's a no. Frangibles were often given to air marshals so they didn't depressurize the plane. They've often been mistaken for hollow-point rounds. On the one hand, the NYPD, as a rule, didn't hand out frangible rounds or hollow-points. And D's collection of guns in our trunk didn't come with any.

Alex parked the car, and we entered together. Once we were inside, we clipped our badges to our belts and we suddenly just became two more cops on the scene. The civilians didn't want to see us and hoped that we didn't see them. We pretended not to.

I generally make fun of the asylum city concept. I think there's a balance between "deport everyone" and "let everyone stay." Since I wasn't in politics, I could not affect any change on a policy level. Personally, the latter concept had devolved to a point where defying immigration laws included letting actual rapists and murderers go free. That and only that had kept Rene Ormeno out of jail and in the city.

In this particular apartment complex, if ICE hit it, it would have been half empty from the time they started the raid until end of watch.

But that wasn't my problem right now. Alex and I took the elevator, and we pressed the button for the top floor. We got out on the top floor, and I took a deep breath. There was nothing evil on the floor. There was barely a hint that Ormeno was even in the building.

From there, we walked down the stairs.

The smell didn't really catch me until the fifteenth floor. Once it was strong enough for me to get a lock on it, I looked to Alex. "He's definitely here."

Alex sighed. "Damn it. Of course he is."

He reached for his holster and undid the snap on it. He had gotten too close to the demon once. He wasn't willing to take any risk with someone as close to the demon as Ormeno.

"The last thing I need is to be caught in a firefight between you and whatever fresh Hell might be unleashed on us *this* time."

The scent led us to the 13th floor. I grabbed the door, and Alex rolled his eyes. "Of frigging *course* it is."

I smiled. I had never known him to be superstitious, but after the first demon and a few zombies, I couldn't blame him.

I stuck my head out into the hallway for a quick peek. No one was there. They were all trying to avoid the police. It was one of the only two reactions I had ever seen to murder: either the surrounding area came out to play tourist, making it a social event, or they avoided cops like we carried a plague.

I strode out, gun in hand. Alex duplicated me. We walked casually down the hallway. Our guns were held low, behind the thigh so it wouldn't be that obvious. One of the last things we really needed was for someone to open a door and see we were carrying. After that, there was no telling what would happen next.

I sniffed until the foul odor led me to an apartment. Apartment 1313.

Alex said it perfectly before. *Because, of course, it was.*

I stood before the door and raised my foot to kick it in.

I smashed the door open with one good kick, nearly knocking it off its hinges.

I came face to face with Rene Ormeno. His face was even more covered with tattoos than the last time I'd seen him—probably to signify his imprisonment in the mental ward. He was a stout fellow, a few inches shorter than me. It looked more like he had spent 24/7 pumping iron in a prison gym than strapped to the wall of a padded cell.

Before him were a dozen gunmen, on one knee, gun ready.

Ormeno smiled. "Surprise, *pendejo*."

Alex grabbed me and yanked me back as the gunfire started. He held my collar in one hand as he tossed a grenade in with the other.

I drew my gun and called out over the bullets, "I thought we were leaving the heavy weapons in the trunk."

"We said guns, not grenades!" Alex yelled back.

The barrage of gunfire continued, unabated until the grenade went off. *I guess they didn't notice the grenade at all.*

The explosion rocked the floor of the apartment building. We had braced for it, so we wheeled into the apartment doorway immediately after the grenade went off.

We held our fire. The gunmen had all been in the way of the blast. I went right, Alex went left. We swept the apartment, just in case someone was in another room. Everyone in the apartment was dead.

But there was no Ormeno.

The central window was broken, but the panes on either side were undamaged. I ran to it and looked out. Ormeno had jumped from there to a guy-wire outside. He gripped the wire with both hands, then hauled himself up, onto the wire, and started running along it. No one saw him. Not only were we at the back of the building, away from the more eye-catching and entertaining crime scene, New Yorkers never looked up.

"Damn," Alex said at my side. "Parkour running? I didn't think that would ever catch on."

I holstered my gun, my eyes locked on Ormeno. "You take the stairs. I'm going after him the quick way."

Alex gaped at me. "You can't be serious. Did you see that drop? I—"

Alex grabbed me again and pulled me down behind a couch. Automatic gunfire slammed into the furniture, punching holes above our heads. Alex casually pulled out another grenade from his jacket, pulled the pin, flipped out the spoon, and waited a few seconds before casually hurling it over the couch.

It went off, and we sprung up, guns drawn. We made it to the doorway and peeked out, guns first.

Every door in the hallway was opening, and MS-13 gunmen poured out. It was like Ormeno had already known how D had laid out his security at his Bayside apartment and duplicated it.

Of course, I thought. *It's enemy territory. He had to have a strong presence. Otherwise he'd be screwed when the Latin Kings came around.*

"Too many," I stated as I opened fire.

Alex and I pulled back as the entire hallway opened up in gunfire.

Alex pulled out two more grenades.

I gaped and looked him up and down. "How many of those do you have?"

"Six."

"Why?"

He gave me a look as he pulled out the pins. "Given the last time we dealt with your supernatural crap, I'm taking no chances."

Alex backed up, then hurled a grenade in either direction down the hallway. "Only problem is that I don't think I have enough grenades."

"And Ormeno is getting away." I frowned. That window was just so big and open and inviting. And I had levitation abilities ... from time to time. This time, I wouldn't even be asking for much—less "levitation" and more "slow descent."

I grabbed him by the arm. "Come on. We have to go."

Alex looked at me, looked at the window and looked back. "You are *not* taking me out through that window."

I jerked my head back towards the hallway as the grenades exploded. "You'd rather face all of them?"

Alex frowned. He stared at the apartment door. "Maybe."

I grabbed him around the stomach, lifted him off the floor (I was big, he was skinny) and ran for the window.

"Tommy, I'm going to get you for thhhiiiiissssss—" he screamed as I leaped through the broken window with him in tow.

Our Father who art in Heaven, Hallowed be thy name—

My levitation kicked in four floors down. By the time I touched down on the sidewalk, we had slowed enough so that it felt like I had jumped in place. The area was still relatively clear of people. Given the neighborhood, I was relatively certain that it was devoid of security cameras—especially if Ormeno and his crew were in the area for any length of time.

"I think I need adult diapers now," Alex muttered.

I placed Alex down on the sidewalk. "I'm after Ormeno. Keep up if you can."

I turned towards Ormeno and ran. I was able to track him by smell from rooftop to rooftop, even though I was still on the street. I dodged around pedestrians, jumped over mailboxes, jump-kicked over a bike courier, then leaped onto a telephone pole with grips for climbing. I partially levitated my way up the pole, going from handhold to five handholds up. I leveled off with the tallest fire escape and jumped from the pole to land on the escape's guard rail. I leapt from there right onto the roof, turning after Ormeno.

Ormeno, meanwhile, leaped from roof to roof, taking a straight line the entire way. Nothing stopped him or got in his way. He cartwheeled in the air over an HVAC unit as tall as I was. He smacked his hands against the flat side of a roof access door and used that and his momentum to vault onto and over it.

I figured he was in trouble when the next roof was blocked by the gap between two streets. It was at least four lanes wide.

Ormeno jumped. As his arc began to descend, he somersaulted in the air, kicking out towards the next roof.

And he landed without a scratch.

How the Hell ... exactly.

I ran faster and tried to pray harder. This wasn't requesting a little extra distance, nor was it asking for gravity to not kill me when I hit the pavement. This was a prayer to virtually carry me across 96 feet of traffic lanes, parking lanes, and sidewalk, as well as bringing me down within the low wall surrounding the roof.

I will lift You up, O Lord, for You have lifted me up ... I suspect no one ever meant the Psalm quite that literally.

I ran for the roof's edge and sped up. *O Lord my God, I cried to You for help, and You healed me. O Lord, You have brought me up from the grave. You have kept me alive so that I will not go down into the deep.*

I jumped.

Chapter 10

BAD DOG, NO COOKIE

I didn't clear the street.

I didn't land on the roof Ormeno jumped onto.

I overtook the street and landed right on top of Ormeno.

I slammed Ormeno to the roof. Pro wrestlers would have approved of that body-slam. He went sprawling as I flattened him. His hands were outstretched as though he had deliberately prostrated himself. I grabbed Ormeno's hair with my left hand, and drove my right forearm into the back of his head, grinding his face into the roof.

"How did you do it, Rene? Huh?" I elbowed the back of his head for emphasis, then pressed my sharp elbow into his skull. "How'd you recover from being driven insane by a *demon*? How did you really get out of the nuthouse?"

Ormeno pulled his hands in, as though he were going to do a push-up. I based my legs around him. I was more than willing to hold on no matter how much bucking he did.

"I've been upgraded, *esse*," he rasped as he shoved off of the roof.

We went *flying* back. He and I came a good ten feet off the floor before we started to come down. On reflex, I twisted in the air, putting him face down on the roof again.

His legs shot out for the roof, and he landed hard. It didn't seem to slow him down from shaking like a dog, trying to dislodge me. My arm whipped around his neck, and my legs wrapped around his torso.

Maybe I should have had my gun out while I was running. I could put a bullet into him now and be done with it...

Because that won't get a website taken down, you idiot. You need him alive ... even if only to disprove that he's not the one who put a hit out on you.

Ormeno charged for an HVAC unit, bending at the waist so that I would take the brunt of the damage. I reluctantly let go. He stopped before he got to the HVAC and spun.

For the first time today, I met Ormeno's eyes.

They were glowing a bright, fiery red. And this wasn't "the light caught his eye, and his pupil held a little red flash." His entire eye socket looked like they were filled with fire. The next thing was for his head to explode and become one giant flaming skull.

He grinned at my slack expression. When he spoke, I could hear not only his voice but the dark echoes of other voices, other forces, each one more dissonant than the other. Each voice spoke in its own dark tongue and its own horrid curses, and each voice was a different type of pain.

"I told you to watch for the warlock," Ormeno taunted. "You didn't listen, Tommy. Too late for you. Too late for *everyone*." He threw his head back and laughed like a lunatic. "This entire city will burn!"

I reached for my gun. Ormeno reared back and punched into the HVAC system. He twisted back to me, hurling the unit fan like a discus. I drove forward, towards him and under the fan. I came up in his face, driving a right hook into his nose. His head snapped back and recoiled instantly. It was perfectly placed for my left hook, followed by my right backhand. I reversed my left elbow, driving that into his face. I segued that into a left hammer fist into the side of his head. I followed that up with a punch to his throat that should have either crushed his windpipe or send his Adam's apple into his mouth. Either way, it should have sucked for him.

Ormeno laughed.

I performed a flying knee, driving my knee right into his mid-thorax. I grabbed both sides of his head and screamed, "The power of Christ compels you, you sonuvabitch!"

The fire in his eyes dimmed, and he roared in pain. He grabbed my shirt front and threw me away, nearly across the roof. I slammed into the roof gravel and skidded into the wall at the roof's edge.

Ormeno fell back, grabbing his head in pain. He gave a feral growl, raised his fingers to his lips, and whistled like he was calling a dog.

Then I heard real growls. Two of them, from two directions.

Wolves. Powerfully built wolves the size of a large draft horse, with ebony fur and burning, fiery red eyes. The roof smoked where their paws touched the gravel, as prints of flame burned through the stone.

Ormeno waved at me with a lunatic smile as he backed up. "Don't play too rough. Hellhounds can bite."

Ormeno fell backwards, off of the roof, and I was certain that it wouldn't be the last I saw of him.

I didn't wait for the hellhounds to do anything. I made it to one knee, then drew both of my guns—from the hip holster and from my backup at the small of my back. I dual-wielded my weapons, pouring lead into both wolves.

The bullets smacked the wolves at multiple points—head, eye, neck. They staggered back under the impacts, but didn't fall over. When the slide on both guns locked open, the wolves shook their heads as though they shrugged off water.

They opened their mouths at the same time and roared... only the roar came out as a stream of white-hot flame.

I leaped back, on top of the HVAC unit, then dropped behind it before it became too hot to be near. I dove to my right, making sure to keep moving as I reloaded.

Lucky I did. One of the hellhounds smashed right through the HVAC system like it wasn't there. Red-hot metal flew everywhere. It roared again, and I dove over the edge of the roof.

Thank God I landed on a fire escape. Considering that the wolves were on fire and I needed to escape, I couldn't think of anything more appropriate.

The wolf howled in rage. It's gigantic footprint slammed down onto the roof edge. I scrambled to my feet, bracing for impact.

The wolf's muzzle came over the edge of the roof, jaws agape and drooling acid that steamed when it landed and burned a hole through whatever it touched.

I thrust my gun forward into its open mouth and emptied the magazine.

The wolf sagged and dropped to the roof, out of my sight. I ejected the magazine and reloaded. *Next time, I'm bringing the MP5. No matter what.*

I rammed the magazine home and slid the chamber back in time for the next hellhound to smash through the wall around the roof. I fell back as it slashed for my face. Its claws barely grazed me, but even that opened up three huge welts in my left cheek. I slammed on my back against the fire escape landing. As I stabbed my gun at the hound and pulled the trigger, I reached into my right-hand suit jacket for a flask.

The bullets didn't do much against this hellhound. It kept coming through the hole it made. I kept pushing myself back with my feet, sliding along the escape.

It slowly closed with me. It was either angry enough that it didn't mind the bullets, or tough enough that bullets didn't phase it now that it had a taste for them. Either way, it didn't stop closing.

My back pressed up against the rail for the fire escape. I was out of room. I pulled the flask out and opened it with my thumb.

"Nice doggie," I said. "Want a drink?"

I splashed the hellhound with holy water.

The hellhound's fur burned while it fell back. It cried and whimpered at the attack. This time, I stood up, leveled my gun at its eye and fired, emptying the rest of the magazine. It took the right eye from the monster, snapping its head to one side.

It growled, faced me, and lunged forward. I sidestepped to its blind side, smacking it over the head with my gun. It reared back, claws in the arm, roaring in both rage and pain.

That's when I delivered a roundhouse kick to one of the back legs touched with holy water. It was a low kick, close in. I drove my shoulder into its side before it crashed to the fire escape.

It instead went right over the side, crashing down to the street. It landed on its back.

I saw the wounded creature struggle to rise again. But it was too late. One of Manhattan's many construction trucks smashed into it.

I turned, double checking that the other hellhound was truly dead. It was in mid-immolation. If it even had any bones, they had burned away.

Thank God they're self-cleaning. Otherwise, we'd have a really hard time explaining this.

Chapter 11

GOING TO WARLOCK

"So, what the Hell, Tom? Is Ormeno possessed now?" Alex nearly yelled in my ear as we drove away from Spanish Harlem. "Do we have another freaking demon to battle? I don't want another demon. If we have another demon, I am going the Hell home and holing up with my shotgun."

I let Alex rant for a while. There was no way we would make a speedy getaway from Spanish Harlem. It was still Manhattan. Bumper to bumper traffic stopped only after midnight. The mayor's idiotic regulation that made twenty-five the mandatory speed limit for the entire city made it even worse (Supposedly, it's better to be struck by a car going 25 than 30. Yeah. Sure).

But we made it to Broadway and headed south.

Why south? Why not? It gave us time to plan our next move by driving the length of the island. And since I wasn't in a rush, I drove in the slow lane and let all the other cars on the road fight each other.

Why Broadway? Because it runs the length of the island. It's also so crowded that it would take even more time.

I needed that time to think.

I didn't know the answer to Alex's questions. Ormeno didn't exhibit the signs of being possessed. There was no speaking in tongues. There was no telekinesis. There was nothing that added up to the traditional signs of being possessed. No extra voices.

If you discounted his eyes of flame, acting like he was scorched when I started rattling off a line from the rite of exorcism and that he summoned Hellhounds.

You know. The little things.

Despite his newfound powers and abilities that made me nervous, the only thing I had to go on was Ormeno boasting about "the warlock." Since that technically didn't help me worth a damn, I had to do some mental math.

Unfortunately, it meant I had only one other place to go that made sense. And it was probably going to end badly.

Everything tied together. It had to, if only because Ormeno was involved. The demon sent one of his legion into Ormeno. The cult summoned the demon. The cult even picked one of their own members, a serial killer, to house the demon. When I last chatted with Ormeno in his padded cell, he linked the warlock to the cult.

The only conclusion with the facts to hand was that the warlock was the primary adversary in this case. She, he, or it was out to get me —since it was typically a male pronoun, that would be my assumption. The warlock probably had a hand in breaking out Ormeno from the nuthouse. If I were to make a guess, *if* Ormeno *wasn't* possessed, Ormeno had been granted a few powers and abilities by said warlock.

Then again, I hadn't considered that I could be located by a Jamaican street gang with access to zombies and scrying tools. But at this point, I had a hard time believing that I was surprised. Really, the past year had been just that insane. Now that I knew that the mumbo jumbo wasn't limited to cults and demons, I had a whole new set of concerns. It was bad enough when I had to worry about gangbangers with armor-piercing rounds. If this stuff was so easy to access, that almost any random idiot could scry my location or summon zombies, or God knew what else, I was in trouble.

And no, not "my fellow cops." I meant me. Because this Dark Web bounty put me on the radar of every street tough with an ability out of a D&D spell manual. What was next? Vampires? Werewolves?

Bounty hunters who threw fireballs? Why not? After all, eye of newt didn't grow on trees, right? Wizards gotta pay the bills, don't they? Werewolf grooming was expensive, right?

At that point, I didn't know if any of that was a joke. A brave new world of occult powers opened up before me and dumped all of its various and sundry henchmen in my lap.

"We're going to have to talk with the Deputy Mayor," I stated suddenly, interrupting Alex's rant.

Alex stopped and stared at me a moment. He didn't even notice when a taxi cut us off. Then again, I barely noticed. It was the fifth one. "We're going after Baracus? About freaking time. I hate that guy."

I paused, surprised. We'd been on our guard for months after the battle in King's Point, but there hadn't been much to talk about. Sure, we knew that Baracus was a bad guy, but what could we have done about it? We kept an eye on him as much as we could. But unless he broke the law, the only thing we could do was outright assassinate him. And when one considered that we had thrown someone who looked exactly like him into a fire pit a previous evening, we didn't even know what would have put him down.

Alex killed some free time every week or so trailing Baracus, but nothing creepy showed up. Baracus didn't hang out in cemeteries. He didn't spend time around livestock for animal sacrifices. He didn't steal from little old ladies. He didn't mug anyone. Murder anyone. He didn't even jaywalk, apparently.

Again, all of that meant nothing. See above for "we threw him in a fire pit." I didn't think he was fireproof—if he had been, I would have expected him to crawl out of the pit on fire to try to kill us. If he wasn't fireproof, that meant there must be two of him. At least two. Technically, Alex could have tracked Baracus until Hell froze over and never have gotten anything. After a few months, Alex believed me and stopped.

However, all that work paid off for one excellent reason.

Alex already knew where Baracus lived. Funny enough, he didn't even live in New York City. His home was in Monmouth Beach, New Jersey.

Or, as Alex put it, "He lives in freaking New Jersey. That definitely makes him evil."

I rolled my eyes as I corrected course for New Jersey, heading west.

Alex immediately objected. "No. Keep going south. We'll go through the Battery, then take the BQE to the Verrazano, then Outerbridge."

I frowned at the suggestion. The route he suggested took us the entire length of Manhattan Island, then going southeast through the Battery Tunnel into Brooklyn. This would lead to the southbound Brooklyn-Queens Expressway, then west again over the Verrazano Bridge into Staten Island. At the other end of Staten Island was the Outerbridge crossing into New Jersey.

I simply wanted to go west through the Lincoln Tunnel, into New Jersey, then straight down I-95 until we had to follow the shoreline to Monmouth.

"You have a good reason for that?"

"The least amount of time in Jersey, the better."

I sighed. Most New Yorkers didn't like New Jersey. Woody Allen once summed up the attitude perfectly in his classic line, "If Jersey is the punchline, you don't need the rest of the joke."

I drove on, content to go Alex's route. Considering the traffic, it wouldn't make a difference either way. I went down the FDR Expressway, on the East side of Manhattan, taking us along the river.

I spotted a sign stating that speed and the highway were monitored by drones. It was a new policy instituted by the mayor to suck the last penny from the population, while at the same time cut out police officers. There was a reason the NYPD turned our backs on him.

... Wait a second. Drone patrol here all the time. So who would notice one more?

"You don't think someone could send a drone after us, do you?" I asked Alex.

Alex looked at me. "Have you seen how big some of our drones are? They're about the size of a dinner plate. Okay, go big, a very large serving platter. There's no way anyone can send a drone big enough for offensive abilities."

I frowned. I looked in my side view mirror and adjusted it upwards. Right on time, there was a drone. And Alex was right. It was about the size of a dinner plate. It wasn't that big. The only way it could harm us was to crash into the windshield and drive us off the road.

Then it sprouted wings of fire.

And a flaming dragon's head.

And a tail made of fire.

The drone had served as the base for some sort of spell, one that turned it into a fiery wyvern.

I pressed my foot down on the pedal. *As long as it didn't crash into us, we're fine, right?*

The dragon-shaped fire avatar reared back its head before spitting out a ball of flame as big as our car. I jerked to the left, dodging the explosion that cratered the highway.

"Alex. We should have taken I-95."

Chapter 12

HIGHWAY TO HELL

The fireballs came fast and furious. I didn't ask about how the construct could have generated that much fuel for the flames. It was magical crap, and I didn't even have the slightest inkling of how that sort of thing would work. At that moment, the only thing that kept us alive was the Grace of God. Mostly because I had problems believing that even my reflexes were good enough to keep up with the massive attacks.

After a moment of chinking around cars, zipping through traffic and at one point deliberately letting a garbage truck take the full brunt of a blast, the explosions stopped coming. I spared a quick glance just to see if the drone had exhausted its ammunition.

It still flew behind us and now changed tactics. Instead of the mouth breathing fire, the wings re-angled. It was almost like...

A fighter making a strafing run. Damn it.

The next thing I knew, small lines of fire a foot long punched through the air, pelting the car roof and truck, and the cars around us. A taxi lost control and swerved into us. It slammed us into the barrier that kept cars from going into the East River. The taxi sped on as we slowed down. The next round of literal fire anticipated where we would be next, based on our rate of speed from before the impact.

The next burst was a massive one-shot fireball that hit the yellow cab. The taxi went up in a bright phosphorescent white globe.

The taxi, the driver, and both passengers were all consumed. The only thing left were the two rear tires, which rolled on for a few yards before falling over.

Okay, that's it.

I shifted tactics. I slammed down on the gas and headed for the nearest exit. It dropped me out into the middle of York Avenue. I sped along, going west instead of south. The drone would have to circle around and come back to reengage a lock. I chinked south down First Avenue.

For those of you who don't know, First Avenue is a one-way street that went north. Any New Yorker knew that.

I hoped that whoever was guiding the drone was from out of town.

I drove over the sidewalk, slamming down on the horn the entire way. When I turned south, I didn't even bother crossing the street to do so. So on top of driving on the sidewalk, I was on the wrong side of the road, too. The right side mirror collided with that of another parked car, ripping it off our car.

Civilians scattered, many jumping onto the hoods of parked cars or into businesses. I slammed into garbage cans, mailboxes, and I clipped one tree still strung up with Christmas lights all year round.

"Don't like the way I drive," Alex muttered, "stay off the sidewalk."

Of course, some New Yorkers being the way they are, still didn't look up from their smartphones, even as I slammed down on the horn the entire way. I had to chink right at one point to avoid several teenagers who didn't have the survival instinct that God gave a baby duck. I took out an entire rack of rental bicycles. (Yes, really. Welcome to New York.) I swerved back in time to avoid taking out an entire crowd of tourists just standing on the corner, waiting for the light to turn. You could tell they were tourists because they actually waited.

I ground the side of our car against the parked cars. Alex cursed, inching towards me and away from the door.

The automatic fire poured down again, strafing the cars we were up against. It had locked onto us again. It was useless to keep going the wrong way down a one-way street. I muttered a prayer and took the next left.

We were now below Fiftieth Street, so there was no more York Avenue. We were back on the FDR. Since the shootout started, traffic behind us had stalled. *Some* New York drivers had survival instincts, and most of them had hit the brakes the moment the drone opened fire. This meant that the FDR was clear. I opened up the engine and really started speeding.

We shot into the UN Tunnel. While it took us under the United Nations building, it wasn't strictly a tunnel. There were a series of pillars on the East side of the road, keeping the UN campus from coming down onto the expressway. The fire drone disappeared from our mirror, not anticipating an obstruction at that elevation.

"Come get us, you son of a bitch," I muttered. "Come on. Where are you?"

Alex grabbed the chicken handle above his cracked window and ground out through clenched teeth, "Don't taunt the supernatural fire drone. It might hear you."

"You want to do something? Shoot at it."

"With what? My nine? I think that will only piss it off."

I glanced at him. "You have two grenades and a trunk full of guns. Think of something."

He was about to argue some more when something silenced him.

The fire drone had sped ahead of us, swooped around, and came in the other end of the tunnel.

"Duck!" I barked as the bullets of fire lashed out. They punched through the windshield in front and out the back. One or two of them cut through the windows and sides of the doors, collapsing the roof almost on top of us.

Alex raised his pistol and blind fired at the wyvern drone.

I had a slightly different thought.

I reangled the car, making it slightly off-center of the road, drifting towards the barricade separating the north- and southbound traffic.

The wyvern drone corrected its course to intercept me. Its mouth opened wide, large enough to clamp down on our car. Since it didn't have a stomach, there wouldn't be enough of us to fit in a matchbox.

The drone's mouth turned white hot. We'd be disintegrated.

It flew so close to the street, the road liquified.

As we closed, it didn't even bother to shoot at us anymore. Why bother wasting the effort? We came straight for it.

Before we got too close, maybe within fifty feet, I jerked the car to the left even more. We slammed against the concrete barrier and bounced off of it at a forty-five-degree angle.

Away from the mouth of the wyvern drone.

We drove right under the wings of fire. The fire was so hot, it distorted the air around it. The only thing that saved us was what little remained of the roof. It had absorbed the heat, turning into red-hot metal.

Alex punched up with the muzzle of his gun, finally knocking the roof off of the car. He turned around in his seat and opened fire at the construct.

The bullets melted before they could reach the drone in the center.

"At least it's going the wrong way."

The fire receded for a moment, leaving only the drone.

The dragon head, wings, and tail sprouted out again, facing us. This time, it roared.

"Drive faster!" Alex bellowed as he dove back down into his seat.

I slammed the pedal down to the floor. "This is as faster as I can go!"

We shot past the East River Ferry and grabbed the first exit. One of the nice things about the FDR is that it was elevated, with a street and parking underneath it. I tacked back under the expressway, giving us some cover. It might be able to melt bullets, but did it want to try smashing through concrete?

Unfortunately, that only gave us cover to Thirtieth Street.

We smashed through the chain-link fence. "Any sign of it?" I called over the wind, now that our car was a convertible.

Alex poked his head up. "Not yet. But it'll get us soon."

I didn't wait for the drone to find us again, but I made a right, then a left quickly thereafter.

I drove us through a playground.

The Asser Levy Recreation Center has a long, wide parking lot that connected 25th Street and 23rd Street, just off of the FDR. I shot out from there, crossed 23rd without looking (would *you* look at this point?) and sped into a private residential development, Stuyvesant Town—Peter Cooper Village. It was off of Gramercy Park, with Mt. Sinai-Beth Israel hospital on one side, the FDR on the other. It was a nice, cushy, upper-class complex with a great view of the East River, within walking distance of the Water Club.

It also had internal roads surrounded by tall buildings. So unless the drone was guided with someone scrying at the controls, we were clear.

We came out at the StuyTown end around 14th Street, coming out on Avenue B, in the East Village's Alphabet City.

We were going straight through Manhattan, while the FDR circled the island. Once we had broken line of sight with the drone for over 11 blocks, we had probably lost it. If someone were scrying for us, we wouldn't have been able to keep it off of our backs for that long. The only way it could reestablish contact would be if the pilot got lucky or if they knew where we were going.

I had a sinking feeling in my stomach that didn't discount that possibility.

We made it through Brooklyn and over the Verrazano, into Staten Island. I made a point of staying on the lower level of the bridge. There were few ways into New Jersey from Manhattan. It was a coin toss about whether or not we stayed on track. Backtracking to go through the Lincoln Tunnel would eat up time we didn't have. Neither one of us wanted to go through the Bronx. If they knew we were going to head to New Jersey (a not unreasonable assumption, if Ormeno had called in and reported to Baracus what he told me), then it was a roll of the dice for both our pursuers and us about whether or not we would intersect. If they scried for me, then it didn't matter which route we took.

The road leading into Staten Island was packed with the usual mix of passenger cars and trucks. It was a gray, overcast afternoon, and traffic was everyone who wanted to get home or get out of the city. The trucks all headed to I-95 and southward. The cars were going everywhere.

Once we were through the toll booths, I had a sudden empty, dread feeling in my guts. I pressed down on the gas as though we were already being pursued again.

Alex exclaimed as he was suddenly thrown back in his seat. "Hey! What's the matter? Is the Balrog back?"

"Look," was all I told him as I sped around a truck.

Then the truck exploded, flipping over on its side, jack-knifing into the middle of the highway and blocking traffic.

"Don't think I need to," Alex said. "Drive faster."

I tapped a button on the car radio. The song that played? It was from a group called Within Temptation. The song was entitled *Faster*. We were in the midst of the chorus, which repeated "faster and faster" about four times.

I took the hint. As I sped up, the fiery drone sped into view of the rearview mirror. It was about twenty feet above us. I was doing 95 miles an hour. It was catching up.

The teeth in the dragon's mouth slowly turned white. Whoever guided the drone wanted to take no chances. It was going to come in and clamp down on us. The jaws would snap shut and reduce us and the car to so much slag. Forget dental identification; there might not even be enough of us left for DNA.

I went faster.

So did the drone.

I called to Alex over the wind. "How's your throwing arm?"

"Why?"

"I need you throw a grenade."

I explained what the drone was doing. I explained what I was going to do.

Alex roared, "Are you nuts?"

I jerked the car to speed under a highway sign. The drone struck it and burned a hole right through it.

Alex frowned. "Okay, fine, let's do this."

The song continued. We were in a guitar solo near the end. The drone closed in so much that the "Objects in the mirror may be closer than they appear" warning was less and less a comfort.

The song stopped.

Then so did I. "Now!" I barked, stomping on the brakes, pulling the emergency and sharply turning the wheel, putting the car into a fishtail.

The drone shot past us, unable to stop fast enough.

Alex threw his second to last grenade.

He missed.

The grenade sailed off as the drone looped back, twisting around to fly level in a perfect Immelman loop. It came back. Only this time it was at cruising speed. We were stopped, facing the wrong way on the highway, blocked off by a truck at one end and the drone on the other. The drone sprouted legs and touched down. The feet burned holes in the tarmac. Its entire mouth turned white-hot.

"Screw this," Alex muttered, and hurled another grenade without even pulling the pin. It went right for the dragon head.

The dragon cocked its head to one side, and the grenade went right past. The head reared back, ready to strike.

"This is gonna hurt," Alex muttered.

The fiery dragon head shot forward, mouth open wide.

The grenade completed its arc, falling straight down onto the drone.

The white hot jaws closed on us.

The flaming construct around the drone set off the grenade. The point-blank fragments and the concussion ripped the drone to pieces, scattering it all over the road.

The jaws, the dragon, the wings, everything, blinked out of existence.

Six feet away from the car, there were scorch marks from where the dragon's mouth had been a split second before.

"Cut it closer next time, why don't you?" I asked.

Alex fell back in his seat. "I freaking hate New Jersey."

Chapter 13

DRAG ME TO ... NEW JERSEY?

Monmouth Beach was the nice part of New Jersey. Driving along the road nearby was an ocean view and the open air. Call it the land of small business owners or the moderately wealthy. There was a yacht club. If you couldn't find the neighborhood, then they didn't want you. But despite that, the security boiled down to the local cops. There were no fences, just really aggressive bushes. The houses were large but stopped short of mansions.

Monmouth Beach was a borough of Monmouth County. It only had over 3,200 people living there. It was basically a small beach community on the Jersey Shore. Victorian houses and multimillion-dollar homes filled it. Unlike Staten Island, when Hurricane Sandy ripped through, these homes were repaired. The entire borough was only a square mile. It also had two lovely little beach clubs and docks and yachts.

However, our barely functioning car would stand out anywhere short of a junkyard.

So instead of taking a direct route down 36, which would have taken us around the shoreline (and bottle-necked us on a series of bridges) we went down the Garden State Parkway and hung a left.

That brought us up the other side of 36, through a lesser neighborhood called Long Branch. We parked around the back of a Home Depot, out of sight and behind crates of potting soil.

"Now what?" Alex asked.

"Now, recon. We walk."

We each took our turn in the back of the car. We pulled the back seat down to access our trunk of weapons. One grabbed a backpack and loaded up while the other stood watch. I went for the MP5, sound suppressor and plenty of rounds. Most importantly, I grabbed a knife. I didn't want to make a lot of noise. The sound suppressors were nice, but if I needed to open fire, they weren't going to help much. Not only would other people be shooting back at me who would have an advantage of having loud guns, but sound suppressors didn't silence anything. "Silencer" was a terrible misnomer. A sound suppressor merely reduced a gunshot from an explosion a foot or so away from your head to the noise level of a jackhammer ... only a foot or so away from your head.

We were able to get there within an hour on foot. We didn't run, but took our time. The ties were left in the car. We would have left our jackets behind as well, but we didn't want our guns hanging out.

The home of Bokor Baracus was a nice piece of real estate, with about an acre of property. The narrow side of the house faced the road, while the actual front of the building faced a long driveway. The backyard was on the other side of the house, where most of the property was. It was only a two- story house, but long enough for two houses. The doors were all French, which seemed insecure ... but then, he had people for that.

Alex and I casually walked by twice, with fifteen minutes in between. There were three guards in front, another three at the opposite side, and we estimated that there were probably another four in the backyard. For a house that big, there would be at least an additional five inside, maybe as many as ten.

There were also no security cameras around the house. Probably for the very good reason that they didn't want a visual record of what went on in the house. Lord knows that if I practiced what Baracus did, I'd want a jammer for all things video and audio.

As for the smell...

I had never been to a body farm. My father's father had both been to the first body farm and was old enough to remember when Secaucus NJ was the home of area pig farms; he said they smelled like body farms. They were places where forensic experiments happened all the time. Corpses would be left in multiple different environments with endless variations in their situation. Does the body decompose differently in fertilizer or potting soil? Sand or mud? Freezing temperatures? Boiling temperatures? Which insects will get to the body first in this or that environment?

To me, the house smelled like death itself. The smell of evil was what I suspected a body farm would be like if all the corpses were left outside in the worst heat and humidity.

"Dinner?" Alex asked as we passed.

I sniffed the air again. I was able to breathe. "Amen to that."

"Pun intended?"

"Shut up, Alex."

We stopped in at a local Chinese takeout place near our car. We sat in a corner while we chowed down. Since we hadn't stopped to eat all day, we were both starved. Though we had been running on adrenaline so long, we hadn't noticed.

Alex waited until we were fully served before he asked, "So, what do you think is the point of all this?"

"How so?"

His voice dropped to a harsh whisper. "I like you Tommy, but you're not worth ten million dollars."

I shrugged. "I am to somebody."

"But if MS-13 isn't behind this warlock, and this warlock is the one putting up the cash, then what does this guy do that he can burn the cash? What does he get out of you being dead?"

I frowned. "When the cult came after me, it was simple revenge. They didn't like that a Catholic had thwarted their plans."

Alex shook his head. "Doesn't work. What exactly was their *plan*, man? Seriously, they released a demonic outbreak in Rikers Island. Two thousand demonic inmates let loose in the city. What happens when they hit the street? Riots and blood. Yeah. Sure. But how does that benefit *anyone*? *Cui bono?*"

Who benefits? "I have no idea. There wouldn't be a private security company who could take on all of New York. Maybe someone calls in the National Guard? Then what? Why bother?"

He jabbed his plastic fork in my direction. "Exactly. Ten million. Think about it. What ties everything together? Demonic infestation of a *city*? Maybe a lot of people start going to church again."

I snorted. "You think that the Cardinal started his fund drive to up attendance in church with a plague of demons upon the city? Seriously?"

Alex shrugged. "I've heard dumber ideas. Not sure from who but someone, I'm sure."

Considering our target was a deputy mayor, I had to ask. "What about the mayor? Any way to guarantee that he'd profit?"

"Only if he really wanted to see the city half destroyed. Normally, I'd say money but how? Real estate will drop like a stone, and the property values would be dramatically lower. But what happens after that? There's no way in Hell anyone would move into the city. Thanks to the internet, whole companies could afford to relocate out of the northeast to where everything was cheaper. Real estate would become worthless. Besides, if his concern were money, he could get a thousand guys on your ass for a six-figure bounty. Why ten million?"

I nodded. "And if he's really a warlock, would money be his primary goal? Magical abilities aren't something you associate with someone working from a Lex Luthor playbook. And vice versa." I leaned forward. "So we have two problems. First: what was the original plan? What do you get with a death cult and a demonic outbreak in New York City? Second: how could anyone benefit from my death? It has to be more than revenge. As you said, revenge can be had for cheaper than this. After we have a chat with Mister Baracus, we should ask Father Freeman. He should know if there's some sort of supernatural benefit or side effect of killing off someone like me."

Alex nodded as he dug into his food. He chewed thoughtfully for a long moment. "Did you ever get around to asking him about warlocks in general?"

"No. Why should I? It's not exactly like he can add anything. Warlock. Bad guy. Evil wizard. What more do we need to know? Any abilities he might have, we'll probably have to discover when we engage him. Which will suck, but still, we can't know until we engage him. Her. It. We're going to have to do what we usually do. Ask questions."

Alex sighed. "Yeah. Sure, Tommy. Because he'll answer if we ask nicely."

I frowned. "He's a bokor. I'm not even certain cutting off body parts would help. This also assumes that the Baracus we're looking at is going to be the Baracus we need. It could be another double."

Alex shrugged. "So? We'll get something out of it. Even if we just toss the place. There should be *something* in the house. Even if he just has a complete set of corpses in the basement."

I rolled my eyes. "Don't even joke."

"Who's joking? For all we know, the guards on patrol are zombies with good makeup jobs. Speaking of which ..." Alex drifted off.

I leaned forward. "Yes?"

He leaned over to meet me halfway. "Lethal force?"

I frowned. I wasn't adverse to it. But there were problems.

On the one hand, these could just be simple paid security. They could be cops in plain clothes, sent to protect the deputy mayor.

On the other hand, if they were minions of the warlock, or the walking dead, they were going to be a pain in the ass. Stealth and lethal force would be the best way to tackle them. Sneaking up behind one of them and running a knife into the brain would be the best way to handle them.

"I think I have a plan."

BOTH ALEX and I slept in the car. I had barely caught my breath since the crooked SWAT team broke into my house that morning, a mere 18 hours ago, and I needed to catch up on my sleep.

Unfortunately, I had problems sleeping. Not surprising. But the more I tried to calm my mind, the more I had to dwell on the mystery of who the warlock was. It had to be Baracus or Hoynes. But because they worked so closely together, it was impossible to get a definitive conclusion. And yes, everything that Hoynes did felt like enemy action, but that was politics. I agreed with him and his part on nothing. Ever. At all. Yes, Hoynes released Ormeno from jail, but that could have been motivated by a hatred of me and a love of criminals. Yes, Hoynes accepted money from the Women's Health Corps, but he ran on the Democrat ticket, and they were abortionists, so they were inseparable. In fact, there was nothing about the evidence that made Hoynes any more or less a suspect than any other Democrat in New York City politics...

Except for Bokor Baracus working with Hoynes on a daily basis. But if Baracus was the warlock and not just a bokor, would he lower himself to working for a mere politician? Would he tie himself down like that? Or was Hoynes merely a puppet that Baracus used while following his own agenda? If Baracus was the real power behind the throne, then Hoynes was a patsy. Maybe not an innocent patsy, but a patsy.

As I went around and around in my mind, along the line, I eventually fell asleep.

The alarm I had set on my phone woke us after midnight. It was a deliberate choice. It meant that fewer people would be on the street, and most people would at least try to be going to sleep.

We walked back to Baracus' house.

Alex was the first to approach the home. He had his badge out and held up as he approached, waiting for the guards to see what he was holding.

One guard reached for his radio after seeing the badge, but Alex shook his finger at him to wave him off. He crooked his finger, beckoning the guard toward him.

The other two guards came along, flanking the first.

The lead guard stopped within six feet of Alex. "What do you want..." he looked at Alex's badge. "Detective?"

"I want to talk with the Deputy Mayor."

The guard didn't so much as blink. "No."

Alex tapped his badge. "This says that—"

"That you can go back to New York."

The guard reached behind him for a gun.

I darted out from the bushes behind the three guards. I had knives drawn. I swung the knives together like I was trying to bear hug the two gunmen. The knives drove in the temple of each of them. They fell over like I had hit their off button.

Alex, on the other hand, jabbed up with his knife, which he had opened while talking to the guard. He jammed it underneath the guard's chin.

My plan was easy. If they tried to kill cops who openly identified themselves, the guards were probably evil. I would have sniffed them out, but the entire area around the house smelled like evil.

I pulled my knives away from the dead guards, then wiped the blades off on their clothing.

I pulled away one of the knives, and skulked to the left side out the house, the end that faced the street. I slipped into the bushes that acted as a gate between one house and the other.

I came to the end of the flora as I neared the back of the home. A guard stood there, submachinegun armed and ready.

He had his back to the bushes.

This time, I didn't hesitate. I clamped my hand over his mouth and stabbed him in the kidney. Before he could die, I reached around his front and slashed his throat. It was overkill, but if that didn't kill him, I'd have to worry. I spun the corpse around to prevent the arterial spray from covering me, dropping the body back in the bushes I came from.

The back of the house had a nice little open patio with overhang, for people who liked having tea during a rainstorm or something. The remaining two guards stood a few dozen feet away from the deck. The lights were on under the patio, which provided them with a little light. Both of them seemed bored. They didn't even bother to keep actively surveying. They just stood there. They weren't even patrolling. It was like they thought they were backup for the guards in front.

I walked along in a crouch. I closed in on the nearest guard while keeping my eye on the guard farthest away.

Without warning, the guard I closed in on looked at his watch. He turned to his right, walking over to the other guard. I dropped flat, hoping that the dark of the night would camouflage my gray suit.

The two guards talked to each other for a moment. Then the first guard went into the house, leaving the second one alone, which would have been perfect, except he decided to patrol now, covering both positions. He kept his eyes up and level and steady, fully alert.

But most importantly, his eyes were on the property line, not on the ground.

He stopped three feet away from me, eyes ahead of him.

Three slashes of my knife to his femoral artery, jugular vein and kidney made short work of him.

I dragged the guard along the grass, bringing him closer to the house, keeping him in the well of darkness created by the nearby porch light.

"Yo. Morgan. Where the hell are you?"

I froze. The other guard had come back.

He was looking away from me, and I took a chance, charging right for him.

Unfortunately, I'm not a sprinter. I'm taller than average and had eaten up a lot of my running time going after Ormeno. The guard heard me clomping towards him and whipped around to see the charging rhino coming right at him. He didn't waste a breath calling for help, but he made the mistake of reaching for his gun.

The Tueller test is a training exercise to prepare against a short-range knife attack when armed only with a holstered handgun. It was named after Sergeant Dennis Tueller of the Salt Lake City Police Department who wondered how quickly an attacker with a knife could cover 21 feet. He timed it as 1.5 seconds. With training, the armed gunman could draw down on the knifeman.

The guard obviously had never done a Tueller drill. I crashed into him. My left hand clamped down on his gun hand as he reached the pistol. I body-checked him, bringing him crashing down to the patio. All the air in his body was forced out as I landed on him.

My knife arced and drove into his temple. I twisted it in a little, and his eyes went wide and still.

I grabbed the body and rolled off the patio with it, into the dark.

I waited for nearly a minute before I texted Alex to come and meet me in the backyard.

Alex showed up another two minutes later. He looked at the corpse next to me, and his eyes widened. "Geez, Tommy. For a saint, you've got a heck of a body count."

I tried to shrug, but the adrenaline was kicking in. "Xavier Loyola was a soldier. Granted, that was before his life-changing conversation. Come on, let's get inside before someone figures out the door was open too long."

Chapter 14

SYMPATHY FOR THE BOKOR

Alex and I quietly swept through the house. It was a nice house. At one end was a connected pool house. The kitchen was all marble with an island counter in the center. The living room was more like a lounge. The dining room was big enough to comfortably host twenty.

The strange thing was that there were no other guards. None. If they weren't on the first floor, they weren't going to be anywhere else in the house, which was bizarre, at the very least.

I swept back through the house, working back towards the central stairs, when Alex fell into the kitchen through the other end, thrown.

And there stood our target, Bokor Baracus. The Deputy Mayor for Social Justice stepped into the doorway, filling it. He wasn't so much broad as he was tall. And he was *tall*.

I didn't care. I drew on him. "Freeze, sucker. We need to talk."

I couldn't even make out his facial features. But when he smiled, I could see each gleaming white tooth.

"I do not think so," he said in his deep, lyrical Haitian accent.

On my right was a soft *click*. I spun into a crouch. Another gunman had appeared within feet of me. I fired three times—two to the head, one to the heart. I turned back to Baracus, but a knee was already heading for my face. I barely had enough time to throw up my arm to block the strike.

Even with the block, the impact sent me sprawling. I slapped the floor with my hands and swung my legs over my head, adding to the momentum. I came up on my feet. My gun only came up forty-five degrees from my body when Baracus clamped his hand down on my arm, locking it in place.

He smiled right in my face. "*So* good to see you again, Detective Nolan."

I bounced on the ball of my foot, springing up with my knees, driving the crown of my head into his mouth. His head recoiled, but his hold on me didn't break. He whirled around, lifting me off of my feet, slamming me into a French window.

"You think you can come to *my* home!" he roared as he yanked me close. His right hand clamped over my throat. The unholy, malicious gleam in his eyes bore into me as he slowly closed his long fingers on my throat. "You think you can defeat *me* in my place of *power*? How *stupid* must you think me be?"

Alex groaned from the kitchen. He was slowly making his way to his hands and knees. He still had his weapon in hand.

Baracus snarled and hurled me at my partner. We crashed into each other and went down in a tangle. Baracus was on us in an instant, kicking both of our guns away. He reached down and grabbed each of us by the throat. He had me in his right, Alex in his left. With an ease that contradicted his slender frame, he hauled both of us off of the floor. We dangled in the air as he slowly choked us.

"I would ask why you came, but I don't think you have the *time!*" he said with a manic laugh that shook my skull.

My left hand went up and over his hold on my throat, wrapping my fingers around his thumb. This was the standard anti-choking procedure. Breaking the grip would normally be easy. The victim being strangled didn't need much-added room to breathe. And four fingers versus one thumb almost always worked.

However, Baracus was a bokor in name and in deed. The unnatural strength of the undead ran through him as if he were Franken-stein's monster.

But my hands were free, leaving me able to bring up my knife from my belt and slice into his forearm.

Baracus dropped me with a shout of surprise. He was immune to pain. He was immune to death. But he wasn't immune to the laws of body mechanics. Slashing his forearm had cut the muscles operating the fingers. Even if he were a zombie, he needed those muscles to close his fingers.

I shot in, driving the knife up into his armpit, forcing the tip of the blade into the shoulder joint. He screamed in pain but couldn't swipe at me with his free arm. He tried to swing Alex at me like a club, but I bent my knees, dropping into a crouch. As I dropped, I slid my knife down his ribs and all the way to his hip. I pulled back the knife and drove it into the inside of his right thigh, just above the knee but below the femoral artery. I twisted the knife in his leg, then shot forward, dashing behind him.

I dragged my knife along the way, slashing open his thigh muscles.

Baracus' right side collapsed. He let go of Alex so he could grab onto a counter. Alex was still conscious enough to stagger back, remaining on his feet.

Since I didn't know how long he would even stay wounded, I grabbed a fry pan hanging on the wall and swung it down onto Bara-cus' head. He swayed to one side.

It wasn't the damage the pan could have done. I used an old wrestling trick meant for metal folding chair shots to the head. The crown of the head was tougher and harder than the sides, meaning that a wrestler could dent a chair with his head, but still be upright without a massive concussion.

I couldn't risk that.

I planned to be in and out quickly, not with Baracus. After our first confrontation with him, we couldn't tell what the upper limit of his strength was, making restraints pointless. Even breaking bones wouldn't work if he healed quickly.

And we had no idea what reinforcements were at his beck and call. If he had revenants in the basement or zombies on speed dial, we needed to be there and gone again quickly.

Since we couldn't take him with us, he needed to remain conscious.

We grabbed the knives from the kitchen block and proceeded to pin Baracus down like a butterfly. Except instead of wings, we drove knives behind his kneecap and pinned him to the floor through the shoulders.

We were not surprised when Baracus didn't cry out or bleed.

I stomped on his chest, not to hurt him, but to add to the restraint. Alex stepped on his hand, keeping that pinned as well.

"Are you the warlock? Did you put the hit out on me?"

Baracus looked at me a moment, then laughed. This is not a sound I'd expect from someone pinned to the floor with cutlery through joints. "Is that what you think? I am not your Warlock. I serve a different master." He moved as though he shrugged, but the blades kept him down. "I merely consult."

"Is that what you were doing with the Women's Health Corps?" Alex asked. "Consulting?"

Baracus bobbed his head from side to side, again, as though he were shrugging. "After a fashion. I set up their Moloch worship." He looked at Alex. "Some people must pay frequently for their power. They may pay ahead, but even that may run out. They paid frequently to keep ahead."

Alex looked at me. "He talks quickly. I didn't think he'd be this chatty."

Baracus scoffed. "Oh, please. I personally have no loyalty to this Warlock. None of us ever really have any loyalty. We will all turn on each other eventually. We don't even need a supernatural leader or source. Ever see Communists? Nazis? They slaughter their *own* people by the score."

I didn't know at the time if it was nerves or supernatural prodding, but I felt the need to hurry. "How about we go into this convoluted plan of his?"

He gave me the sweetest smile. "Whatever could you mean?"

I pressed down on him with my foot to get his attention. "The warlock's plan. Death cults. Demons. Prison riots. What the Hell? Isn't all of that a little convoluted?"

The Bokor shrugged again—or tried to. "It's not really that convoluted. It takes a lot to destroy a city."

I filed that away for later. Pressing him for minute details seemed like a waste of time. "And what about the hit? Seriously, I'm just a cop doing my job. I didn't have anything on you. I didn't have anything on the warlock. Putting a hit out on me is just overkill."

Baracus sighed. It was the exasperation of a consultant who knew better than the employer but had been ignored. It was an "I told them, but they never listen" sigh. "The Women's Health Corps – ha! – overreached when they took their revenge on you. They failed. And while the warlock I work with has paid for his power in advance, it is hard to keep up the payments. It is especially difficult when one burns through power and no longer has a mechanism for sacrifice."

I nodded, tracking along with this insanity. "Where do I come into it?"

"Ah, you, Detective Nolan? A *prophet*? One who could become a *saint* when he died? One who has thwarted the forces of Hell not once but *twice*? You are more valuable than you can imagine. *You* will pay the warlock's debt in full. Your death may not come at his hands, but it does not need to. He merely needs to *arrange* for it."

I narrowed my eyes. "Damn it. Alex, get our guns. We need to get out of here."

Baracus blinked. For once, we had surprised him. "What? Didn't you want to ask anything more? Is that all you wanted?"

I wanted to tell him that we had all we needed. I wanted to tell him that answering our questions would cost us time we didn't have. He may not have had any loyalty to the warlock, but the longer he talked, the longer we were in one place. We had already cleared the floor of gunmen, yet someone had nearly jumped me.

"We don't need you anymore."

Alex took me at my word, came back with our guns, and stomped the Bokor in the head. He looked at me. "Don't we need to know who the warlock is?"

"We do know. He's underneath one person, working for one guy."

Alex arched his brows. "The warlock is Mayor Hoynes?" He shrugged. "Huh. It explains so much. No way a guy that incompetent wins elections."

That's when the doors blew in, and the vampires attacked.

Chapter 15

DARKNESS FALLS

The French doors at the front and the back of the house blew in. Alex and I dove behind the kitchen island. Bullets flew from both directions, tearing up the kitchen. We couldn't see anything, and we could barely hear each other over the noise.

"Maybe we should have gotten the Hell out of here," Alex screamed over the bullets.

One of the attackers jumped over the island and landed between us. He ignored Alex shooting him in the back, reached down, and grabbed me.

Then his hands burst into flames. He roared and fell back. His eyes turned yellow, his teeth extended into fangs, and he hissed like Christopher Lee in a Hammer film.

I sprang forward (not up, I didn't want my head blown off) and grabbed him by his belt. His waist started to smoke. I yanked him into the island and shoved him over. It burst into flame, and he went up like flash powder.

I unslung my backpack and pulled out the MP5 submachine gun. "I guess that was a vampire."

Alex looked up from his own backpack, blinked, then nodded. "Sure. Of course. Why not? They're allergic to you?"

"Apparently." Because why not? "Alex, we have to—"

Alex sent a grenade sailing over the kitchen island and the rear doors, and hurled another one towards the living room in the front. When the grenades went off, he leaned around the kitchen doorway and fired.

I bobbed up. The dining room was cleared of people still standing. Some were zombies torn apart by the grenade. Some were creatures I couldn't identify.

However, the real problem was the gunmen still out in the backyard, firing inside with automatic weapons. They were all heavily-tattooed Hispanic men.

In the midst of them was Rene Ormeno.

"Seriously, why can't he get a hobby?" I muttered to myself as I fired in three round bursts. One of the gang thugs dropped. I ducked immediately as they all focused on my muzzle flashes.

Alex patted me on the shoulder. He pointed out the front. I arched my brows. He spoke at me, but I couldn't hear him. This time, it wasn't over the bullets. I couldn't even hear the bullets.

A fist punched through the floor from the basement. The hand was covered in a black glove, and the arm was covered in tattoos.

I fired into the hand as I jerked away from it. More hands burst through the floor. Instead of us, they were near Baracus. They reached over and jerked out the knives pinning him to the floor.

They were freeing him. *Crap.*

Alex reached over and slapped me on the arm. I read his lips as he screamed, "Now!"

This time, we both threw grenades at the back door as we ran for the front. We ran through the living room and burst through the ruined French doors. Explosions ripped through the house.

Only more men stood out at the edge of the driveway. They stood there in black, silent and patient. One in the middle gave a little wave and smiled, flashing teeth.

More specifically, flashing fang.

I smiled this time and ran for them. Alex fired off bullets behind me, and I felt them rattle my ribs.

The vampires closed on me as I ran for them.

I raised my fist, ready to strike. They didn't even consider moving away.

Dear Lord, I really want that last thing to not be a fluke.

I punched the lead vampire right in the face.

His face burst into flame, devouring his face, then the rest of his body. He was gone in a bright white flash.

The other vampires exchanged looks. One gave the same exact little wave as the previous one.

Then they disappeared. I allowed myself a quick laugh and a smile. *I guess I won't have to worry about vampires anymore. At least not this time out.*

I spun to face the driveway, to see what Alex shot at.

MS-13 tried to circle around the house and come out into the driveway. Alex had them stymied for the moment. I grabbed two more grenades and hurled them before I opened fire as well, driving them back.

You might be wondering, *How have they not been hit yet?* With all of that lead going through the air, most people would think that it would be easy for at least *one* bullet to hit us.

To which the answer is, have you ever held a gun?

To start with, ignore what you see in the movies, unless it is, perhaps any *John Wick* movie. Any moron who holds his gun sideways at a 90-degree flip is begging to miss. Brass flies everywhere, even into the eyes, and that's just if you're holding it properly, in two hands. In this case, they fired from the hip, which meant that they were barely aiming.

Second, shooting is a skill that you have to hone. Most importantly, you have to hone it with the individual weapon. This requires lots of practice. Unless they were firing their own personal weapons they had never held these weapons before tonight. The guns had probably been stolen and shipped in for the occasion. They'd probably never fired them (where would you fire them in New Jersey? The nearest farm was miles away, and they had shown up within minutes), and thus could never hone their skill with the individual weapon.

Third, controlling a weapon on full automatic is a pain in the ass if you're doing everything *right* with a weapon you know like the back of your hand. The recoil would be a pain in the ass on a good day. They were less shooting for us and more shooting in our general direction, hoping we'd get hit.

It's why most drive-by shootings only work at relatively close range; when the target doesn't see it coming, and the shooter isn't busy being shot at.

Fourth, they burned through ammunition like water on a hot day. Full automatic fire meant that they fired at a rate of thousands of rounds a minute.

As for Alex and myself, we had spent hundreds of hours on the range, firing as many bullets as we could afford. And, while we were firing guns we had never used before, we were firing on semiautomatic, one bullet at a time, and *we were aiming.*

On top of that, we backed up into the dark, unlit street. Flames and lights from the house backlit the gang members. The only thing I could think of at that moment was a prayer to the patron saint of artillery.

St Barbara, you are stronger than the tower of a fortress and the fury of hurricanes. Do not let lightning hit me, thunder frighten me, or the roar of canons jolt my courage or bravery. Stay always by my side so that I may confront all the storms and battles of my life with my head held high and a serene countenance. Winning all the struggles, may I, aware of doing my duty, be grateful to you, my protector, and render thanks to God, the Creator of Heaven, Earth and Nature who has the power to dominate the fury of the storm and to mitigate the cruelty of war.

I suddenly caught a stronger smell of evil than from just the property. I turned left, gun coming with me.

The stock of the MP5 landed squarely in the hand of Rene Ormeno. He ripped the gun out of my hands as he backhanded me, sending me flying into the street. He carelessly tossed the SMG in the other direction. He had come around the property, over the flora separating Baracus' home from his neighbor's. If I hadn't smelled him, he could have come up behind me and snapped my neck like a twig.

I landed in a roll, coming up with my handgun.

Ormeno closed, grabbing my gun wrist and twisting my arm, shaking the weapon out of my hand. I was a little surprised that he hadn't broken it. His eyes were dimmer than before.

Because I was praying.

I head-butted Ormeno. *Saint Michael the Archangel, defend us in battle—*

Ormeno growled and let go of me like I was a hot frying pan. He backhanded me. I staggered, but my head was still attached. My feet never left the ground.

I growled. "Let's dance."

I burst in to meet Ormeno. He swung a roundhouse punch, but both of my arms shot up. My left came up in a boxing block, so his fist landed in my bicep. My right lashed out in a cross to the face. The strike rocked him. I grabbed his right shoulder with my right hand and the same arm at the wrist with my left. I pulled him down into a knee. I threw two more knees before he blocked with his left forearm. I kept my hold on his wrist but raised my right arm and drove my elbow down into the back of his neck.

Ormeno dropped to one knee and rolled, coming up to his feet. He pulled his arm from my grip and pushed off the ground, ramming his right shoulder into my chest. I was big, he was bulky. The strike rocked me, but I based out on my right back foot. I clawed his face with my fingers, driving the fingertips into his eyes and my palm into his nose. I drove his head back, making his body bend backwards. My other hand came up, grabbing his forehead, and I twisted on my back foot, throwing him to the tarmac.

Be our protection against the wickedness and snares of the devil. May God rebuke him we humbly pray—

He pulled out a Bowie knife, taking up a boxer's pose.

I pulled out my own knife and was more like a fencer, my empty left hand against my chest. He came in with a teasing high strike. I slashed at it, but he pulled back before it could make contact, and arced down for my thigh. I dropped my arm, bringing it straight down, the edge of my knife only poised to meet his forearm. Ormeno's forearm ran into the edge of my blade, but he pulled back before I could do real damage.

He burst forward, closing with me. His knife came in low, at waist height. My left arm came down in a chop against his wrist, and I brought my blade down, then slashed up, tagging him. My knife came up to my collarbone, the butt of the handle up against my shoulder, the point of the blade aimed right at Ormeno.

I drove my blade forward as Ormeno slammed against me deliberately. His pecs slammed against my arm, so I only drove my knife into his shoulder, not his eye.

—and do Thou, O Prince of the Heavenly Host, by the Power of God, cast into Hell Satan and all the evil spirits, who prowl through the world seeking the ruin of souls. Amen.

So I bit his nose.

Ormeno roared, and I twisted my knife in his shoulder. Since I figured he was more like Baracus at this point than not, I brought my foot up and raked it down his leg, stomping on his kneecap, dislocating it. He fell to one knee, pulling my knife from his shoulder. I backhanded his face with my knife, cutting his face open. He swiped at my legs with the knife, biting into my calf.

I responded by kicking him in the shoulder, pinning him against the street. I kicked the knife away.

"What the hell are you doing, Rene?" I barked at him. "Working with the *mayor*? Are you stupid?"

Ormeno sneered at me. "Who do you think got me out of jail? Who do you think *fixed* my mind? I either work with the Mayor, or I go back to eternal damnation while I'm still alive." His eyes lit with a new kind of fire, madness, and rage. "Where the only cure is *your* presence. I'd rather be under the control of the mayor than you, *jefe*."

I ground my teeth. I was so pissed at being confused for the source of all this odd stuff. "It's not me, Rene, it's *God*. He's with me. *His* presence healed you, you fool. Not mine, you moron. Your motto is rape, kill, control. The mayor now controls you, and after this brief reprieve, when you die, you *really* get to feel what eternity in Hell is like."

Ormeno stopped struggling and paused. He looked at me, confused. This was a new idea that had never occurred to him.

Alex caught up to us, hurling yet another grenade back at the shooters. He slapped me on the chest. "Hey, Tommy, let's go."

From inside the house came a bellow so loud and fierce, it sounded like a kaiju roar. "Ormeno!"

With a jerk, Ormeno yanked his hand from under my foot, rolled to his feet, and ran for the house. He walked with a hint of a limp, but nowhere near a busted kneecap.

"Let's get out of here," Alex said.

I joined him as we ran back for our car. It took me a moment, but I realized that I heard him clearly. It was a surprise, but I realized that I had essentially channeled God's grace to fight Ormeno. He healed my hearing while we were at it. Even my calf didn't hurt as badly as it had a moment ago

God was on my side.

Chapter 16

LICENSE TO KILL

We had stopped in a nearby parking lot as we collapsed the MP5s, reloaded them, and put them away in our backpacks. We sat down on the bumper of a car, and caught our breath as the sirens went by. As the adrenaline burned through us, it was ... fun. I suppose.

As we waited for our heart rates to come down, and for the sirens to fade into the distance, Alex asked, "So, the warlock is the mayor?"

I nodded. "Apparently."

We sat in silence for a long minute.

"Well, that's going to be fun," he snarked. "Why do you think he did it?"

I frowned, thinking back over the past few months. After the incident with the Women's Health Corps/death cult of Moloch, Alex and I had played a trump card against the mayor: body camera footage of some of the Mayor's more insulting comments about his constituents. His approval numbers had dropped like a rock. No surprise there. But since then, his policies still got through. It didn't seem to hamper his ability to get things done. Recently, his poll numbers had even started to rise again.

The policies in question were also getting darker and darker.

Hoynes was in talks with the DA – Carlton's boss – to press charges against the Catholic church under RICO, the same laws used against the mafia. He argued that the Catholic church hid pedophiles. This would have been fine if all of the cases he cited weren't decades old and prosecuting them would violate every statute of limitations on the books. It wouldn't result in the prosecution of any child molester, but it would result in the confiscation of every church in the city and all of their bank accounts, property, etc.

Hoynes offered to keep the prosecutors away if the Catholic church in New York started marrying "nontraditional couples." There was the similar talk of doing the same thing to Orthodox Jews once the Catholic priests were out of the way. Protestants weren't being considered since they were trending towards gay marriage anyway. Islam wasn't even discussed-- neither the politicians nor the activists mention them during these rants.

At the same time, Hoynes pushed the public school system to start sex education in the first grade. The special sex educators consisted entirely of transsexuals and transvestites. The special "education" hadn't started yet, but every mutter of pulling children out of public schools and into homeschooling was met with threats of calling Child Protective Services and sending the police to people's home to arrest the offending homeschoolers. No cop I know would do that, but there were some people in CPS I could see doing that – to their mind, it was easier than investigating abusive parents, and the law-abiding wouldn't put up as much of a fight. Hoynes argued that "I'm a Libertarian! Children should be allowed to make their decisions about sex with all of the information at their disposal. How dare you take away their right to make an informed choice about what they do with their body!"

If you think that there's a disconnect between the public stances of "pedophiles bad" (but shouldn't be prosecuted) and "teach seven-year-olds sex" you're not the only one.

If you're wondering that I should have seen this coming sooner, then you haven't noted the similarities between Hoynes and the political stance of the average Democrat politician. The RICO idea had been suggested before. Using the law to force a homosexual agenda on Churches that didn't want to perform said weddings? Home-schooling had been a target of the left in New York City since the concept began.

And yet, despite fascist methods and pissing off voters left right and center, Hoynes was gaining in the polls. I had always chalked that up to bad polling and the reliability of Manhattan elitists who would vote Democrat even if the candidate had personally threat-ened to kill them all after the election.

But magic and politics?

"I think you were correct back there," I said. "He's too much of an incompetent to really get elected. He's using magic to get things done, manipulate the polls, and probably would use it to get elected again. You heard the bokor. The Mayor needs me dead to pay off his debts to his Friends on the Other Side. Election season more or less starts in a few months."

"Really? He's using black magic to win elections?" Alex asked. He paused a moment. "Okay. Yeah. That really does make too much sense. Any ideas on how to take him down?"

I shrugged. "Prayer and bullets?"

"Why not? It seems to have worked before. Now the real question becomes how do we get to him?"

It wasn't an idle question. The mayor would have some serious security, in addition to whatever powers and abilities he already had. If he didn't blast us with lightning from two miles out, his security detail would fill us with bullets.

Better and better.

"We should talk to ADA Carlton. He's read into our situation."

Assistant District Attorney William Carlton had tripped over the case of the demonic defendant back when this insanity first started. He later deduced my secret abilities by doing more legwork and analysis than I would have thought he'd have time for. We could go to him, and he wouldn't immediately throw us in a mental hospital if we said the mayor was a spawn of Satan. He had a brain that worked better than any three people we knew. If anyone could come up with a way to legally corner the mayor, it would be him.

Except if we could come up with legal tactics, so could the mayor? If he were smart, he wouldn't need magic, though, would he?

At that moment, my cell phone rang. I sighed and answered. "Nolan."

"McNally. Where are you?"

I blinked. I hadn't expected Statler or Waldorf to contact me. "We're out of New York. I wanted my family to lie low while this whole thing blew over." Which wasn't exactly a lie. They were individually true statements. It wasn't my fault if he tied them together.

"You're not in New Jersey, are you?"

"Why do you ask?" Answering a question with a question is a tried and true method of avoiding the questions. Any question.

"There's now an APB out on you. The Deputy Mayor insists that you just tried to murder him. Is that true?"

I hesitated. Not because I was thinking up a lie. I merely thought that they would have taken more time to think of a pretense to sic someone on us. "No. It is not true. Full stop. Do you want the truth?"

"Yes—no. We don't want to know."

I blinked. *We? What we? ...of course. McNally is probably on speaker with Horowitz in the room.* "Say hello to Waldorf for me."

"He prefers to be Statler," he said in a casual, offhand manner. "Listen, keep your head down. You know, and I know that the mayor hates your guts. He's probably using this threat on your life as an opportunity to get you killed. Putting an APB out on you gives any corrupt cop an excuse to shoot you while you're trying to escape."

"There any reaction from the beat cops?"

McNally gave a laugh. "Everyone within earshot gave some variation on 'Go Fuck Yourself.' But any cop who wants twenty million won't hesitate."

I blinked. "I think you remember wrong. It was ten million."

"I'm old, not stupid. Your Dark Web bounty doubled in the last few hours."

The bottom fell out of my stomach. Given some of the things that had tried to kill me in the past few hours, "Dark Web" had taken on a whole new feeling for me. Bad enough that every crook with an onion router could look me up and hunt me down. But that also meant supernatural creatures who wanted my head. Those were probably listed on other sites that no one had seen just yet. Vampire message boards? Why not? They were all coming for me.

And they had to win only once. After that, my friends and family could start petitioning Rome for my canonization.

"Understood," I finally told McNally. "I'll pass the message on.'

"Keep out of the city, Detective," McNally warned me. "Even if you're arrested by a cop who's just doing his job, you won't last five minutes in holding."

"Understood." I hung up, turned off the phone, took out the battery, and stuffed them in different pockets.

The right corner of Alex's mouth turned down in a half-frown. "Great. We're trapped in New Jersey for the rest of our lives, aren't we?"

I shook my head. "We need to get to Long Island, remember? Carlton lives in Great Neck."

Alex arched his brows. "In case you didn't notice, to get to Great Neck, you need a car. To get from here to there, you need to go through half of Jersey, then all of Staten Island or the Bronx, then the length of Brooklyn or Queens."

I rolled my eyes. "We can get there by boat."

Alex scoffed. "You mean the ferry from Connecticut? I'm not sure the car can make it that far."

I sighed. "Just give me your phone. I need to get a ride."

Alex dug out his phone and handed it to me. "Why? Are you going to call an Uber? Maybe they'll take all of the guns in our trunk."

I simply sighed and dialed. "After this, we need to stop by the local church. I think I need to stock up on holy water."

☠

MONMOUTH BEACH HAD VERY nice piers and docks.

Thankfully, we knew someone with a boat.

During the battle with the death cult calling itself the Women's Health Corps, D had brought reinforcements with a boat. In this case, we didn't need a small army to come to our rescue, just someone to drive.

The boat pulled up, and much to my surprise, Nate Brindle stepped out onto the dock. "Hey, Nolan, how are you?"

I blinked. "Good to see you. How's life treating you, post-Rikers?"

He shrugged. "Not bad. I still like your little Jedi trick."

Alex arched a brow. "Jedi trick?"

Brindle smiled. "You didn't realize that your partner was a Jedi?"

Alex shook his head. He went back to the car and popped the trunk. "Come on, let's unload the trunk."

Between the three of us, we had filled a flatbed handcart from the trunk in a few minutes. Thankfully, we had burned through a lot of ammunition, which was usually the heaviest part of guns and ammo.

"So, what's the occasion?" Brindle asked once we were underway.

Alex: "Long story."

"We have a few hours."

"Depends," I started. "Do you want to make a few million? You just have to shoot me."

"Say again?"

We explained on the way to King's Point. He rolled his eyes. "Wow. You got on somebody's bad side. I had heard you were pissing people off while I was in jail, but *boy*, have you got it bad."

I shrugged. "I'm Catholic. My people have been annoying the general population for two thousand years. It's part of the job description. Do deny the Devil and all of his works, especially if his works are current fads."

Brindle laughed. "Only you, Nolan. Only you."

Alex yawned. "Pardon me, but I need a nap. I'm getting too old for this crap."

Brindle waited a moment, then asked, "So, how are you doing?"

I flinched. "I'm sorry, what?"

"How are you doing?"

I opened my mouth, but nothing came out. I hadn't given any thought to how this was affecting me, one way or another. It was hard to believe that this was only very late on Monday night (or very Early Tuesday morning, depending), and that one of my parish priests had been murdered right in front of me only 36 hours ago. While hadn't really known him personally, he seemed like a stand-up guy; Mariel had worked with him at the soup kitchen. I had barely slept. When I had slept, I hadn't slept very well. I had only gotten a few hours when the SWAT team kicked in my door, and a few more hours that afternoon. But I've been shot at on five separate occasions by human beings, twice by Balrog drone, killed two hellhounds and ran a parkour foot chase through Spanish Harlem, not to mention both zombies and toasty vampires.

Sure, I was sleepy and mostly running on adrenaline. Aside from that, I was mostly numb. I should have been scared out of my mind. All the forces of Hell seemed to have a target on my back. But I didn't feel scared. Fear wouldn't help. I could only handle what was ahead of me. For everything else, I could pray.

But now, the mayor was out to get me. Dozens if not hundreds of corrupt cops were probably out to kill me. The forces of darkness knew my name and where I lived. They probably also knew what my family looked like and who they were.

Ever since the demon spotted me, I had been a target in one way or another. The demon wanted to destroy me because he could. It had murdered a friend of mine and a friend of my son's, then tried to slaughter my family in our own home. The death cult wanted me because of revenge. The Mayor, a warlock fueled by the powers of Hell, wanted me so he could pay off his debts to his friends on the other side. Friends were *dead*. Cops were *dead*. Brothers in arms were *dead*.

And for *what*? For *nothing*. Because I did halfway decent things for total strangers. I gave to charities. I served with charities. I occasionally put people up in a spare room when they needed it. Far as I could tell, they were minor good deeds on a good day. These little charities had cost me nothing ... until the demon. Maybe a little time that I could afford. Maybe a little money that I could afford. Maybe some patience, which I could afford.

For *that*, Hell wanted me dead. For *that*.

"You know what, Nate? I feel pissed off."

Nate nodded. "Good. Because you don't deserve this shit, man. You really don't."

I chuckled wryly. I started to feel like Alex. "There's a reason one prayer to God is that we *don't* get everything we deserve. Because who, then, would be left standing."

He spared me a look as he drove the boat. "You, probably."

I rolled my eyes. *Not him, too.* "How do you figure? I figure I'm fairly humble, but not that good."

"You're Catholic, ain't you? Don't you know your Bible?"

I didn't laugh. Honest. "I've heard a few lines. Here and there. I even remember a few."

"Blessed are those who hunger and thirst for justice. The merciful will be shown mercy. The pure of heart shall see God. The peace-makers are children of God. And those who are persecuted because of righteousness, theirs is the kingdom of Heaven. Blessed are you when people insult you, persecute you, and falsely say all kinds of evil against you because of Jesus.

"Tell me, which of these are *not* you?"

I was about to protest. But humility was to be honest about your-self. Modesty was to conceal, almost lie about yourself.

Blessed are those who hunger and thirst for justice ... I was a cop. If I didn't do that, I wouldn't be doing my job.

Blessed are the merciful ... More than a few of my fan club who I arrested thought I was merciful. I didn't argue with them that I didn't have to be a prick about arresting them.

Blessed are the pure in heart ... Pass.

Blessed are the peacemakers ... Technically, I was a peace*keeper*, but I would let that distinction pass.

Blessed are those who are persecuted because of God ... Blessed are you when people insult you, persecute you, and falsely say all kinds of evil against you... Which was exactly the story of the past 36 hours, if not the past year.

*Great is your reward in heaven, for in the same way they persecuted the prophets who were before you...*Again, pass.

Funny enough, Father Freeman hadn't hit me with the facts as hard as Nate had. *Maybe he was worried about me getting a swell head.*

I frowned, thinking it over. I still needed a better label than "Saint." "Prophet" didn't even work. I wasn't prophesying anything. I didn't preach.

Screw it. I don't need a label other than Detective.

Finally, after a long moment, I told Nate, "You have a point."

He nodded. "Damn skippy I do. Now, where exactly am I going in King's Point? You got a friend over there?"

"Not exactly. I know of an empty house."

"How do you know it's empty?"

"I killed the previous owners."

Chapter 17

THE CASE OF THE DEDICATED DA

I had only slightly exaggerated when I told Nathan Brindle that I had killed the previous owners of the house in King's Point. I had merely helped in clearing out the death cult from the house. It had been the home base of the organization that called itself the Women's Health Corps. Nate hadn't been around for the firefight and subsequent slaughter of the cultists. Calling it a slaughter might have been an exaggeration, since all of the dead were armed. However, the gunmen were so pitiful at shooting that it really wasn't fair.

Then they got up and tried to kill us again. I had even fewer compunctions about putting them down.

To say that King's Point is the nice part of Long Island doesn't quite capture it. To start with, you have to find it first. There's a little white-letters-on-green-background sign that meekly says "King's Point," as a way of guiding people who know what they're looking for. But if you didn't know they existed, they do not want you in the neighborhood.

If you're driving by King's Point, along Community Drive, there are plenty of tall, lush trees, covering the very existence of the area. It could be mistaken for all of the flora that covered the sides of highways. There is only the barest occasional hint that there is something behind the trees. At the right angle during the winter, when the trees are bare, you can catch glimpses of fine six-bedroom homes and wide arcing driveways, the occasional brownstone or bay window.

To turn into King's Point is to enter the land of *The Great Gatsby*, Great Neck (instead of "Big Egg"). The homes were closer to old-fashioned mansions than the McMansions that arose in the late nineties. The homes were varied, but many had optional extras. Some had extra pieces of land that made for one heck of a front yard. Some had tennis courts and swimming pools that were jealously guarded by a chain link fence (No barbed wire). At a wrong turn, one could unknowingly drive up someone's driveway, mistaking it for a street. Some homes were cut off from the others by an additional bodyguard of trees, isolating themselves from their neighbors. If one stuck to the outer perimeter of King's Point, one would find that every cul-de-sac oversaw the water. Many of the homes at the end of the cul-de-sac had docks and boats in their backyards.

The gardeners probably made more than I did.

King's Point at night remained idyllic. In areas where the street lamps might be insufficient, the external lights of all the homes lit the streets and the walkways, welcoming any and all in the streets to the town.

It short, it looked nice. Some homes were more obviously wealthy than others, but most were subdued and remained low key, unpretentious and not flashy. For the most part, it was what small business owners aspired to—nice home, nice neighborhood, a place to raise the kids without a problem.

It was here that the dragon's den was parked. I could almost see the truck of baby parts pull up to the house and passing it off as the weekly BBQ party with friends from work, which was sort of true.

The former house of the WHC President was in one cul-de-sac that backed into the water. It was a two-story home, and the backyard leading to the water was cut off by trees and a high fence. The home was brown slate. There were two balconies in the front, and at least one more looking over the backyard.

The house had been beautiful. The few windows that had been shot out had been taped up. There was still crime scene tape around the area. The house itself was still tied up in the courts. The Women's Health Corps had been slowly dissolved as part of a RICO suit. RICO convictions ended in the confiscation of all property involved. There were elements of the WHC who weren't part of the cult —we think—who had been fighting back for the better part of the past eight months. They were desperate to get their hands on everything that the cult had left behind, since they were slowly but surely being shut down. Part of that had to do with the cult, part of it had to do with reports that Alex and I had made during the investigation.

To no one's surprise—especially now—the one thing that held up the prosecution of the WHC was the Mayor, who had been putting all of his political capital into keeping the WHC alive. Honestly, I had thought that the Mayor had merely been a pain in the ass, since the WHC had been one of his major supporters. The more we learned about their connection, the less surprised I was.

But they owned a nice house that now stood empty after we arrested or killed everyone using it as a base. I had gone through it with Father Freeman, who had exorcized the place. I had gone through it with the forensics people, who had taken away everything with human fluids on it. It hadn't been a fun day.

They also had a dock. It was probably how they had brought in a lot of their illegal goods, body parts, weapons, etc.

Nate brought the boat up to the dock. We unloaded the weapons and brought the handcart into the house. He had asked if we needed anything else. We told him we needed a car. He smiled and told us to check the driveway. With that, he left.

We checked the driveway. It was a black Nissan Versa, circa 2017.

Alex laughed. "Seriously, Tommy, what did you do for D that he's spending all of this cash on you?"

I shrugged. "Enlightened self-interest. They've sent people after D twice because of me. If I'm out hunting the one who posted the bounty, it's one less thing D has to do himself."

Alex sighed. "Wouldn't it have just been easier for him to shoot you himself?"

"It's not in his wheelhouse. Besides, I've done him enough good turns for him not to do that. He knows that I'm the best friend he's got who's obviously on the right side of the law. He would have to spend *months* training someone else to understand the truth of the matter."

"I'm not even sure I do, and I'm sure I've been with you for a while."

We took the weapons and loaded what we thought we needed into the trunk. We didn't want to bring *all* the guns and bullets since there were only so many we could carry at one time. Add to that the weight ... also, putting all of our bullets in one trunk was just begging for the car to be blown up.

Then we called William Carlton's home from the house. He picked up on the first ring. "About time," he said in his deep, resonant voice.

I blinked, surprised. "How did you even know it was us?" I asked.

"I have the phone number in my phone. I've had it ever since *New York vs. the WHC* began. I never know when I might need it. Who else would be calling from there except you?"

I gave Alex a look that simply said, "*I told you he was smart.*"

"You can get over here in about ten minutes," he continued. "Maybe less. I'll see you soon. Park in the fire zone."

ADA Carlton lived at 33 Knightsbridge Road. It was a nice, modest apartment building in an overpriced neighborhood, a one brick structure built around a sloping courtyard. Despite every instinct to keep out of sight of the local police, we parked as instructed. It was a forced choice. Parking on the street was packed. There was no other parking unless you were a resident of the building.

We entered the brightly lit foyer. Instead of ringing up to Carlton's room, he waited for us. He was a big man, over six feet tall, with a puffy, snowy white beard. The width of his gut exceeded his shoulder span, but not by much. For his age, he looked good. His was dressed in full pinstripe suit, matching vest, sans tie.

He pushed the door open to let us in. "Come in. Press for the elevator."

We walked inside, and he checked the sidewalk. He closed the door. He caught up to us as the elevator opened. We piled in, and we went up a floor.

"Really?" I asked.

"The stairs are slippery. I wouldn't even use them in a fire."

We followed him to his apartment. The door opened into the living room. There was no television, but couches and armchairs, with a coffee table in the middle.

"Please, sit."

I looked around. "I thought you were married."

"She's visiting the grandkids. I can't even breathe funny, lest this WHC case get away from me. I took a vacation once a few months ago. The case nearly fell apart."

We sat on a couch, at opposite cushions. He took his place in an armchair that looked more like a well-padded throne.

"Congratulations on getting here," he began. "I won't ask how you accomplished it. I may not want to know."

"We did nothing illegal," I replied.

"Good. Though we may not need to resort to questions of what's legal by the time this is over," Carlton answered. "I know large parts of what's going on with you at the moment. I know about the bounty. I know about the APB put on you with the NYPD. Are the two connected?"

I nodded. "To start with, we have a massive problem with the mayor."

"Tell me something I don't know."

"He's a warlock and his Deputy Mayor for Social Justice is a Bokor —a voodoo necromancer."

Carlton slowly blinked. "In which case, I believe we need to start back at the beginning."

We did, starting back with the demon possessing the serial killer Christopher Curran. Carlton had already known about the demon. This time, we tied it together with the death cult. The death cult had been at least backed by Mayor Hoynes. Why back a death cult if he's a warlock? In exchange for power, the mayor had needed sacrifices as payment. The cult functioned as his payment plan. The cult would make sacrifices, giving him power. Currently, the mayor needed me to die to finish off his payment plan in full.

"What happens if he doesn't make the final payment?" Carlton asked.

"My guess?" I asked. "Probably much worse than simply losing power. I'd say he goes to Hell even faster."

Carlton nodded. "Reasonable. So, what was the point of the demon? What were they initially setting out to do?"

Alex and I exchanged a look. "That we're still at a loss for."

"That's a problem. But not an immediate one. If the point of you being murdered is to pay off his debts, why not leave town? Take a long vacation?"

"Because that doesn't end the threat," I answered. I sighed. "Killing me is a quick, easy solution for him and his problem. He might find other innocent civilians to sacrifice."

Carlton raised a brow, skeptical about a sacrifice that would equal me. "Perhaps not so innocent?"

I rolled my eyes. I had apparently skimmed over the important part. "Either way, it means his power will level off. He'll be willing and able to exert more power without risking the bill coming due." I looked Carlton right in the eye. "He might be able to use enough of his own magic to influence the case against the WHC, get them up and running again, maybe even get some of the old cultists back into the game. Then his system of payments is up and running again, and we're back to square one. I'd need to stay gone until he dies of old age or falls down a flight of stairs."

Carlton frowned. "In that case, can't you just bi-locate behind him and shove?"

I paused, taken aback. For a man who was in law, he had been one of the people most for advocating extra-judicial punishment. IE: he'd suggested I kill more people than D has. When we were up against the death cult, he'd suggested murder then, too. But they had just kidnapped my son.

If I didn't know any better, I would think he was trying to lead me into temptation.

"You suggest that to all of the cops you work with?" Alex said, echoing my concern.

Carlton's eyes narrowed, and he leaned forward. "You mistake me, sir, for a knave and a coward. I deal in the *law*. But *the law* has nothing on the books to deal with the level of evil you consistently bring me. The *law* has nothing to constrain a demon. The *law* says nothing about taking baby parts from abortion and burning them in your own fire pit to worship your demonic deity—maybe improper disposal of medical waste, but that would be thrown out on the grounds of religious persecution. Don't give me that look—that's half of my problem in the current prosecution, even though child sacrifice is illegal. You have no idea how much the law means to me."

I glanced to my partner. He gave me a return glance. "Why, Detective Packard, I had no idea that the law meant so much."

Packard, completely deadpanned, answered, "True, Detective Nolan. Why, I do declare!"

Carlton's eyes narrowed. "You misunderstand me. The laws of this country had been designed to restrain the government and ensure freedom to citizens. But Hoynes and his ilk use the law to hurt citizens, impinge their freedoms, all the while remaining immune to prosecution. Hell, some state senators take *years* to convict, even on the worst charges. And that's with normal laws. And right now, the law has nothing—I say *nothing*—that will lock away a warlock with political power. He could throw lightning bolts in the middle of Times Square, and as long as he got the proper permits for a pyrotechnic display and struck no one, we couldn't even prosecute him for a noise complaint. Even if we did have such a law, prove it. Prove to a jury that he is behind a single murder. Behind a Dark Web bounty on your head. Prove that he summoned a demon to stick into a serial killer. In fact, if you could *prove* that he was aware that someone was a serial killer *to* stick a demon into him, that's accessory before, during, and after the fact.

"But you come to me and tell me that the mayor is a magic-using monster. It's difficult enough to prosecute a political figure even *without* mystical magical abilities to cloud men's minds and sway the jury. Voir dire is bad enough without all of this. And you want, what? Legal advice in order to lure him into some sort of trap in which he can expose himself and what laws he *has* broken? All without actually entrapping him? I would say that you were quite mad."

"But, yes, this man is evil. You know it. I know it. We all know it. But I can think of nothing to grasp him with. As of this minute, you can't go near him. You can't lay hands on him. You can't speak to him. There is no way to trick him into a confession. To give me a case that I can prosecute ..." Carlton threw his hands up in the air. "You'd have to tie him to something. Prove that he has connections to the cult or the serial killer—not the demon, the *human* serial killer. Connect him to MS-13 and Ormeno. In fact, tie him to anything. I dare you. I double-dog dare you."

Carlton leaned back in the chair. "As I said, killing him would be best."

Alex growled. "You realize that this doesn't really help us."

I shook my head and pressed down on Alex's shoulder. Getting annoyed wouldn't help us. "No. He's right. This is gonna suck. He's just telling us what we need to do to fix this."

Carlton shrugged. "That's if we keep this between us and the forces that we can marshal. We can bring what to bear? Some cops, some of your gang friends? There are other people out there."

I smiled. I knew exactly what he meant. There was a multi-million dollar bounty on me ... so that meant a money trail, and the effort to hide those funds, which were money crimes. The Dark Web involvement made it a federal crime because the Internet was federal. RICO was also a crime, it was a civil court, so less stringent laws ...

So, there were options.

"But first, we must leave you free to operate," Carlton continued. "We have to get this APB off of you. It gives everyone in the tri-state area a license to kill you. After that, we will be filing misconduct charges against everyone involved."

"Step three," I added, "get the mayor to come after me."

Both Alex and Carlton looked at me like I had lost my mind. "Can you think of something that would look less like entrapment, but as incriminating?"

Then the bullets hit the apartment windows.

Chapter 18

ESCAPE FROM GREAT NECK

I lunged from my seat on the couch, grabbing Alex with my left hand so I could pull him off the cushion. Gravity would get him to the floor.

Then I dove for William Carlton. I more or less tackled him, knocking his chair over and I lay flat on him.

"I'm an ADA," he stated flatly. "My windows are bulletproof."

I said nothing as the next bullet shattered the window and struck the wall behind his chair.

"Armor piercing rounds care little for your windows."

I bounced up to a crouch so I could peek out the windows. The apartment complex was built around a courtyard. To get through the courtyard were over two dozen steps from the street, into the yard, followed by a ridiculously winding path. The shooters were at the top of the stairs, firing from street level.

Inside, heavy footsteps pounded down the hall.

Of course, we left all of the interesting heavy weapons out in the car.

The best tactic to engage the hallway was to meet them at the door... which would work if it weren't for the shooters outside.

The best tactic to engage the shooters outside was to stay at the windows and hold the fort until cavalry arrived... leaving us vulnerable to the men coming from the hall.

The best tactic I could think of was to make a stand in the living room, backs against the wall beneath the window, and hope we could hold out, unless the three of us could retreat to a different room in the apartment.

In short, we were screwed.

When the going got tough, the tough started praying.

I love you, Lord, my strength. The Lord is my rock, my fortress and my deliverer; my God is my rock, in whom I take refuge, my shield and the horn of my salvation, my stronghold... We need a good solution.

Suddenly, without any warning, I was inside and outside at the same time. My vision was the ultimate split screen. I was outside, behind the gunmen. I was inside, still where I was.

I had to move fast in both cases.

Outside, I charged the three gunmen with the rifles. They probably figured they would be at a distance, so they didn't have to worry about engaging many people at short distances. One was set up with his rifle on top of a car, using the roof as a platform. I leapt at him. My hands grabbed the back of his head and slammed it forward with my entire body weight. His skull made a dent in the car. The gunman didn't fall down but merely staggered back. I grabbed him by the shoulders and swung him around, hurling him at the next gunman over. Even the third gunman noticed the attack by now. And I was the most important target—I was the one with the bounty on him.

I called to the Lord, who is worthy of praise, and I have been saved from my enemies. In my distress I called to the Lord; I cried to my God for help. From His temple He heard my voice; my cry came before Him, into His ears.

While the attackers were engaged outside, inside, I took the initiative. I charged for the door. The door kicked in as I was ten feet away. The gunmen tossed something in before backing away. I swatted at it with my bare hand, knocking it back out into the outer hallway. I dove to my right, into the first door I saw, landing on the tiled floor of a bathroom.

The flashbang went off in the hallway, blinding and stunning everyone trying to kill us.

The earth trembled and quaked, and the foundations of the mountains shook; they trembled because He was angry. Smoke rose from His nostrils; consuming fire came from His mouth, burning coals blazed out of it. He parted the heavens and came down; dark clouds were under His feet.

Outside, there was still the third man standing. As they went down, I landed on them and flung myself forward, in a roll. I came to a stop past the muzzle of his gun and sprang up. I drove my left fist into his gut, slamming into his diaphragm. All of the air knocked out of him, I head-butted him, crushing his nose. Then I punched him in the throat with a right cross and delivered a right elbow to the side of his head. He slumped against the car. I grabbed the rifle, ripped it from his hands, and hit him over the head with it.

I turned around and found the other two gunmen getting up.

He soared on the wings of the wind. He made darkness his covering, His canopy around him—the dark rain clouds of the sky. Out of the brightness of His presence clouds advanced, with hailstones and bolts of lightning. The Lord thundered from heaven; the voice of the Most High resounded.

Inside, I got up from the bathroom and charged the hallway. All of the gunmen were blinded and disoriented. I didn't show any mercy this time. I slapped the muzzle of a pistol against a wall with my left hand, pinning it with my right. I brought my knee up, nearly to my chest, then stomped down on the first man's kneecap, ripping it out of place. He roared in pain. I grabbed the barrel of the gun, twisted it out of his grip. Then I slammed it into his skull, muzzle first. I didn't care if it discharged into his head. I twisted in a roundhouse arc and stabbed the muzzle into the temple of the man on my left. The strike might as well have been with a metal rod. His head snapped back so hard, his entire body torqued as he fell. The third gunman, behind the first two, blinked, clearing his eyes. I leveled the gun a foot away from his nose and fired. The brains that blew out the back of his head made the man behind him flinch. I aimed and clicked again, but the gun jammed...

And there were three gunmen still standing.

With great bolts of lightning He routed them. The foundations of the earth laid bare at Your rebuke, Lord, at the blast of breath from Your nostrils. He reached down from on high and took hold of me; He drew me out of deep waters. He rescued me from my powerful enemy, from my foes, who were too strong for me.

Outside, I burst forward, kicking the gunman on top in the head. He fell on his cohort, knocking the gun offline. I brought my foot up, then stomped the gunman in the head, smashing his skull against the tarmac.

Well, that was easy. *They confronted me in the day of my disaster, but the Lord was my support. He brought me out into a spacious place; He rescued me because He delighted in me.*

Back in the hallway, I could either try clearing the gun jam or ignore it.

I reared back with the handgun and hurled it into the face of gunman #4. I took two steps forward and jumped over the three dead at my feet. My fist was cocked back far over my shoulder. As I landed, I led with my fist, knocking his head back and dropping him. I followed through, punching *through* the target instead of striking at it, so my fist was down by my hip when I landed. Gunman #5 was within easy reach, so I brought my fist back up, slamming the meaty part into the side of his mouth. Teeth flew as he fell against the wall. I followed up with a left roundhouse to his kidney. I reached over with both hands, grabbed the butt of his handgun and the portion around the hammer, and lifted the barrel right into his face. I slammed his own gun into his face twice more until he fell over.

The last gunman blinked his eyes clear, and they focused on me as I drove the muzzle of the stolen pistol into his gut. I came up to him, nose to nose, and bellowed, "On the floor, or in a box! Drop your weapon and show me your hands!"

His hands went up so fast, his gun went flying. I grabbed him by the shoulder, spun him to the wall, and face-planted him there.

Alex looked out into the hall as I cuffed the last man standing. "You mean we get to arrest one of them? Wow. Here I thought we were just going to have a trail of bodies from New Jersey to Long Island and back."

"Did you call it in?" I asked.

"From Carlton's phone."

"Great. Let's not be here when they show up."

Alex frowned. "We're going to need more handcuffs."

"We have zip ties."

Alex shrugged. "Sure."

William Carlton looked out of his apartment. He studied the beaten and the dead on the floor. "And you were criticizing me for advocating lethal force?"

I smiled at him as I shoved the thug on the floor. "Just the context you were using it, Counselor."

Carlton nodded. "Come, let's walk and talk. You can't have much time before the locals show up."

He escorted us out the front door. He quickly outlined his legal strategy—okay, less of a strategy and more of a script—and I added a few notes. A lot of things needed to be set up in short order.

Including the hint as to where Alex and I would be hiding.

Carlton scoffed at my suggestions, and I made more than a few. He said, "I've been a lawyer longer than you've been alive. I can handle being subtle."

I made a hurt face. "I can be subtle."

He rolled his eyes back up to the floor above. "I saw you being subtle. When the only tool you have is a hammer, every problem looks like a nail."

"When people are using nail guns at you, a hammer is the only reasonable answer."

Carlton sighed. "In any case, get thee gone. I'll tell the police that I handled them all myself, single-handedly, challenging them all to unarmed combat. Or something."

I laughed as Alex and I made it out of the building. I was still smiling as I got into the car and pulled out.

Alex waited until we were out of the bottleneck that was Knightsbridge Road, then asked, "Why are we sure that Carlton needs to be given a hint about where we're hiding? What about those people who cry a lot to find you?"

It took me a moment to figure out what he meant. "Do you mean scry?"

He scoffed. "Whatever."

"One thing I remember about all of this magic crap—it has problems working over or near water. Or was it salt water? Either way, that's another reason to hang out at King's Point. It's surrounded by water, and the house itself is nearly on the dock."

"Should I ask what books you read that in?"

I smiled and thought I'd tease him a little. "I think it was by Kim Harrison."

"Doesn't she do urban fantasy?"

I merely said nothing.

"We're gonna die."

Chapter 19

THE CASE OF THE DISCARDED DETECTIVE

ADA William Carlton walked into the judge's chambers. The phone on his camera was on so that Alex and I could track exactly what was going on during the proceeding. The video was uploaded to a private internet site on the Dark Web. Because the bad guys weren't the only ones who could use a TOR connection.

Also in the room was Bokor Baracus, and the enemy himself, Mayor Hoynes.

Mayor Ricardo Hoynes was an anomaly for New York City in that he was a semi-(big-L) Libertarian. He was less anomalous in that he was a loudmouth who wouldn't know how to shut up if the city depended on it. Big-Ls, like Hoynes, preached "freedom to think for yourself," then browbeat and bullied anyone who disagreed with him.

Hoynes was, for lack of a better term, a blockhead. His head looked like a rectangle. His skin pallor was mostly gray. His eyes were BS brown, and he kept trying to pass for Hispanic. His claim to fame within the Barrio (Spanish Harlem) was marrying a Miami woman who had backed Castro...and was run out of Miami soon after.

Today, he wore a hideous pink tie with tiny blue stripes, a pale blue shirt, and a gray suit.

"Angry" Judge Jacob Vargas had a full beard, closely cropped, and an eye patch over one eye. His hair was black and left in a crew cut. Vargas was well-known for being regularly pissed off, hated other lawyers, and generally didn't care what other people thought of him. To go before him was to come in prepared to offer no sophistry, BS, or obfuscation. He was perfectly fair. He hated everyone equally. But waste his time, and he was the worst enemy one could ever have.

He gave all of us a hard look, with eyes like obsidian. "What exactly are we doing here? Bill, you better not be screwing around."

"Your Honor, you must know me better than that."

He scoffed. "Don't jerk me around. Most of the lawyer jokes I know are walking the halls. What is this about getting an APB rescinded and an injunction against the mayor?"

Hoynes leaped to his feet. "A police officer tried to kill my deputy mayor last night. For some reason, Carlton's trying to protect him."

Carlton shrugged. "Actually, I didn't know that the mayor's office even had the ability to put out an APB on a police officer."

Hoynes glared at me. "Attempted *murderer*."

Vargas glared at Carlton so harshly I expected the camera to melt and for us to lose visual at any moment. "There is an eyewitness. It sounds like they have more than enough to hang him."

Carlton's tone was so calm, you'd almost think he was ignoring both outbursts. "Except, your honor, this APB came barely 12 hours after the *fourth* attempt on this officer's life. Two of those attempts were made by corrupt members of SWAT and bomb squad. There was even an attempt by the gang unit to go after one of Nolan's informants. All so that they could collect a twenty *million* dollar bounty on Nolan's head from the Dark Web. Putting an APB out on him is an invitation to be killed by other corrupt cops, or criminals with police scanners."

Vargas blinked, surprised. He stared daggers at Hoynes and Baracus. "And he had some time to go to..." He glanced at the brief before him. "Monmouth to assassinate Mister Baracus? Why would he do that?"

"He's insane!" Hoynes insisted. "He's been out to get me for nearly a year."

Vargas went back to Carlton. "Has he?"

Carlton coughed. "What the mayor means is that Detective Nolan released several videos a few months ago where the mayor made some ... unfortunate comments about his constituents."

Vargas paused a moment. Then the beard broke out into a slow, smooth smile. "Oh, yes. All of those entertaining clips about the mayor's opinion about how good aborting the gene pool of Harlem meant crime went down. This is the same cop? Interesting."

Hoynes drew himself up, making an ugly scowl. "Excuse me. That has *no bearing* on the APB. Deputy Mayor Baracus *saw* Detective Nolan try to kill him."

Carlton calmly asked, "How could he tell Detective Nolan apart from the rest of the gunmen?"

Judge Vargas winced. "Pardon?"

Carlton picked out a folder and put it down on the desk. "Those would be the other dead bodies. They're all covered with MS-13 tattoos. And there are bullets all over the crime scene. There were reports of automatic weapons fire and explosions. Are we to believe that the Deputy Mayor was close enough to clearly see Detective Nolan in the dead of night, in the middle of a firefight, with automatic weapons, and come away without a scratch on him?"

Carlton gestured at Baracus, and he was correct. The bokor was immaculate and perfectly dressed.

"Please. If Nolan were *actually there*, I could argue that he was trying to *save* Mr. Baracus. Though lord only knows why he would, given what he's been put through. His family is in danger, there is literally a bounty on his head. But somehow, he made time to get to Deputy Mayor Baracus' just in time to thwart an MS-13 assassination attempt on the Deputy Mayor."

Vargas' eyes narrowed again. "Are you seriously trying to spin that one on me, counselor?"

"Absolutely not. It's poppycock. Given the evidence at hand, we could take the facts as given and spin any story we want out of them."

Hoynes' jaw hung open, while Baracus was cool and quiet. Hoynes at least hadn't counted on the fact that there was no evidence that Alex and I had injured the bokor. They couldn't exactly tell Vargas that we had come in, slashed Baracus with a knife in several places, stabbed major joints to pin him to the floor, and yet didn't have a scratch on him the next morning.

Though to be honest, it looked very much like Baracus had already thought of it and he wasn't surprised Carlton had brought it up.

Judge Vargas' lips pursed, trying to keep in his anger. When he spoke, his voice came out strained and enraged.

"What. The FUCK. Are you *assholes. DOING?*" he roared.

Hoynes' eyes narrowed. He jabbed a finger at Vargas. "Watch your tone with me, Jacob. Or I'll make your life miserable. I'll—"

"*You'll get out of my office before I have you thrown out!*" Vargas roared. "And if you waste one more minute of my time, I'll see you both in lockup for contempt of court."

Carlton merely smiled as he stepped out of the way of Carlton and Baracus. Hoynes gave Carlton an evil look. Literally, his eyes flashed red, with a hint of electrical cracking around the edges. He was pissed off and ready to hurt someone. If the ADA wasn't careful, he was going to be the target of the warlock's rage.

Vargas barked, "Carlton. Out."

Carlton followed the other two. Hoynes whirled on Carlton, jabbing his index finger into his face. "What game do you think you're playing, Carlton? Whose side do you think you are on? Nolan's or the city's?"

Carlton arched his bushy brows. "I am, as always, on the side of justice. And truth. You may not be familiar with either of those concepts. Now, if you'll excuse me, I have a long day ahead of me, followed by a meeting in King's Point, and *then* I get to go home."

The mayor flinched. "Where?"

"Home is Great Neck, if you don't mind. I'm there all the time.

When I can. Now, please, good day. And the next time you want to put a hit out on a detective, make certain your story is straight. Be well."

Carlton wandered off.

BACK IN OUR HIDEOUT, Father Richard Freeman, OP, sat with us as he watched the court drama unfold. Freeman was in his late forties, skinny, with just enough gray at his temples to make him an interesting stunt double for a comic book scientist. He wore his black shirt and white collar with a lab coat over it. He was a bit nebbishy, but what would you expect from someone with three PhDs? In German, he would have been addressed as doctor doctor doctor Freeman.

We had Freeman brought in simply and easily. While I had been worried about his phone being wiretapped, or his movements being monitored, or even the ADA's phone being wiretapped by the unscrupulous, I did something simple: I messaged his pager.

Alex sat on my right, with Freeman on my left. My partner said, "I'm surprised Hoynes didn't Jedi mind trick the judge. That's how he gets people to vote, isn't it?"

The priest shrugged. "Strong emotion is difficult to shift. It's hard to sway someone's thoughts if they're so pissed off that they can barely think. Granted, that means the judge's thoughts were an open book, but the judge knows nothing about us or our plans."

I shrugged. "Technically, I barely told Carlton our plan. They could mind read him until doomsday, and they wouldn't know the full extent of our plans."

Father Freeman leaned back in his chair and studied us. "So, what have you two been up to?"

Alex scoffed. "Busy."

Freeman smiled. "I can imagine. May I borrow Tommy for a moment, Alex?"

He shrugged. "Sure. I'm going to head out to get some food now that the APB is lifted."

Alex left. Freeman said nothing for a long moment. "So, Tommy, what are you thinking?'

"I'm thinking that Hoynes needs to go down. We have some feelers out now. We can consider dropping him in jail. Frankly, I'll look forward to it."

Freeman arched a brow. The corner of his lips quirked up in a smile. "You do realize just how insane that statement is, don't you? There's no guarantee that you'll be able to take him alive. You're dealing with forces that you barely have comprehension of. The levels of power we're dealing with could be ... unprecedented."

I frowned. I knew what Father Freeman was saying, but I had already done some of the math. "I don't know if I'm going to survive this. But we're going to have a few forces at our beck and call as well. If I don't get him, someone will."

Freeman cocked his head to one hand. "I think you missed my point. How exactly do you think you'll get him to stand still long enough for you to put the cuffs on him? For all you know, he could be as powerful as any sorcerer in fiction. He could have the proportionate strength and powers of the Greek Pantheon."

I cocked my head to one side, curious. "Are you saying that Baracus was lying? That Hoynes doesn't need to keep making sacrifices to Hell to keep his powers?"

Freeman shook his head. "No. That part is accurate. Power always costs something. After a while, a single soul will only buy so much power. I looked up the data on Hoynes being elected. Only 22% of New York City voted in that election. Now, 16% of the population voted for him. So we're not exactly saying that he has clouded men's mind over the entire city. In large part, he relied on the natural apathy of most New Yorkers towards their government. But that's still a lot of people and a lot of minds. That makes him plenty powerful. And just because the bokor said that he was running low on power means nothing. He could be lying. Or if not, Hoynes' idea of running low on power could be something very different from yours or mine."

I shook my head. Again, the math. "He has to run out of power sooner or later. If he wasn't in danger of running on empty, he wouldn't be doing this. Why do this now if he didn't need to pay his debts in full? Why not wait? Or better yet, why not kill me months ago? If this were for revenge, he would have done this already. If it's not for power, then the timing is arbitrary and capricious. If our enemy is that fickle, then we already have the advantage. But if I'm right, and he's running on empty, then this might be our only time to force him to run out of power, arrest him, and throw him in jail."

Freeman shook his head. "Now you're just on the point where things will get silly. What guarantees do you have that you'll be able to keep him? Say that his power has been drained enough to prevent him from throwing fireballs at you, or choking you to death. What keeps him from getting out of all of this? Being a warlock isn't a crime anymore. You'd have to get him to confess to actual crimes that are on the books. The assassination attempt on you. Money crimes. Something. Carlton already explained this to you. Because if you can't keep him in jail while the prosecution goes on, there's nothing to stop him from other sacrifices, other payments. He does that enough, he can sway the jury with a thought and be free to hunt you down, and we get to do this all over again. He can even kill someone in jail."

I winced. That was also a consideration. I didn't like it, but I had to consider it.

You may be curious about why I was so hesitant to just straight up murder Hoynes.

I wasn't hesitant.

In fact, my orders were to kill the son of a bitch.

Remember that for me, this insanity didn't really start at the church shooting. It started when an angel awoke me from my slumber, demanding that I smite the agents of Satan. If the mayor didn't qualify, no one did. As a person, he was garbage, and that was before one got into his demonic and criminal activities. To my knowledge, he had no good qualities. Any virtue he'd had was corrupted.

The angel had called me a Judge. They had been warlords in the Bible, who rose up to deal with threats to Israel. The angel had demanded that I smite Hoynes. If I took the statements and orders literally, I was for all intents and purposes God's assassin.

But depending on how everything played out, I knew there was a slight possibility that I would have to settle for Hoynes in prison. For the time being, anyway. I would have preferred it if I could just up and assassinate him, but I may not have gotten that option.

"Let's just say I'll leave it up to God."

The front door opened and closed. Alex came back in with a shopping bag. "I forgot the stuff we picked up last night."

"What's that?"

"Insurance," I told Father Freeman. "We're going to need a lot of it."

Alex smiled. "I also placed the Amazon order for same day delivery, but I'm going to see if I can find some stuff out in the wild."

I blinked. This time, I was confused. "What did you order from Amazon?"

"Aluminum tape, iron oxide dust, and magnesium." Alex smiled evilly. "Something for our bokor friend. He's had two shots at me already. He doesn't get a third."

Chapter 20

ARMY OF THE NIGHT

DA William Carlton showed up as planned, parking outside of the home of the former death cult.

As planned, we brought him into the house ... then out the back, down the yard, and into the waiting rowboat. That house would be no place for a lawyer that night.

As expected, within a few minutes, the first members of the party started to arrive. They came in dribs and drabs, here and there.

Three unmarked police cars showed up, but they stayed outside, parking at the far end of the cul-de-sac.

Ten minutes after that, two large black vans showed up. They parked behind the cop cars. The drivers sported MS-13 tattoos on their faces. They also stayed outside.

"Want to bet that Ormeno is in there with them?"

"No bet."

We waited on the first floor, looking out over our makeshift barricade of furniture. Our guns and ammo were laid out on the couch. We had also raided much of the "collection" the WHC had stashed in the house. There had been no blood on any of them, so when my brothers in blue (and in forensics) had examined them, they decided that the collection wasn't evidence, and left it in place.

Which meant that, in addition to the shotguns, SMGs, handguns and rifles D left us, we were also now in possession of a small armory of edged weapons. Both Alex and I had gone for katanas. Because katanas were cool, sharp as hell, and probably something that could even take down a bokor.

We waited as they waited. There was no reason we could think of for the corrupt cops and MS-13 to hesitate. By all rights, they should have come out of their cars and engaged with us.

Then the big rig showed up. It was huge. Massive. I was almost afraid of what could have been in it.

Then the passenger got out of the cab, and I didn't even have to wonder.

It was Bokor Baracus.

The black vans with the MS-13 soldiers opened. Only Rene Ormeno got out.

The lead car for the corrupt cops opened up, and one person got out. It was no one I knew.

"Let's get this party started," Alex said.

I concurred.

I grabbed the bullhorn and said a little prayer. Once I knew that God heard and answered my prayer, I keyed the bullhorn.

"This is Detective Thomas Michael Nolan. You have one chance to surrender and give yourselves up. If you put your weapons on the ground and surrender peacefully, I can ensure that no harm will befall you. If you decide to engage, we will have no choice but to meet you with deadly force. This will be your one and only chance. I suggest you consider carefully, lest you make the wrong decision."

Ormeno, Baracus, and the cop exchanged a look. Baracus shook his head, Ormeno scoffed, and the cop smiled. They weren't going the surrender.

Which was fine. I didn't want them to.

The angel that had awakened me from my sleep, before the SWAT team had tried to murder my family and me, had called me a Judge. It had called me a Prophet.

Both were titles of biblical warlords.

And most importantly, the angels had told me to smite the agents of Satan. These people had decided what side they were on. More important than anything, they hadn't sided against me. They sided against the One whose side I was on. Ormeno knew this. His men must have known this. And the cardinal sin of any cop, one which we all knew in our bones, was to kill another cop.

The mercy of God required I at least make the offer.

I had multiple plans. Each of them had been keyed to my specific abilities. Why? Because I didn't want to so rely on God answering to my every whim that I took Him for granted. I had never once relied on God saving my ass because I didn't want to treat these genuine miracles like magic missiles in D&D. Each miracle was a gift from God. And while Jesus Himself noted that if you harass God enough, he will provide (okay, that's one way to read Luke 11: 5-13), I wasn't going to tell God that "I want X to do Y."

My prayer as a grabbed the bullhorn was simple: *God, grant me what I need to do your will.*

I had bi-located outside. While I talked, distracting them, my double outside went through plan A.

I slipped hand grenades into the wheel well next to the gas tank of each car.

My double had disappeared (reabsorbed?) before the first explosion.

The cars with the cops disappeared, killing all of the corruptibles in blue. The flames even caught the one who stood outside.

The grenades for MS-13 didn't even get a chance to blow up. The ignition of the gas tanks from the first cars had created a fireball that ripped through the first van, flipping it onto the second.

The explosion of the second MS-13 van smacked the cab of the truck to one side. The cab twisted and landed on its side before it too exploded. The trailer tipped over, falling in the street.

The trailer doors burst open, spilling men out onto the street. They had been stacked in there like cordwood. They each came out, armed to the teeth, with a variety of automatic weapons. They were dressed in camouflage gear, war paint on, each of them in full kit.

Professional killers.

I looked a little closer, at their eyes. Each of their eyes had a milky film over them. Their eyes were always straight ahead, locked on the house. It took me a moment, but I figured out what they were. All it took was for me to look at Bokor Baracus' face-splitting grin.

The gunmen were all revenants. They had all probably been well-trained soldiers when they had been alive. Their bodies had remembered what their souls had forgotten.

I turned on the external floodlights. "Shoot for the head, Alex."

"When don't I lately?" he asked, and opened fire with the M4.

I opened fire. The M4 was in my hands, with the shotgun right next to me. We fired on full automatic, but unlike the firefight in Monmouth, we aimed from a stable platform. And using rifles to fire across the street might as well have been point blank range. Besides, we had only so much of each type of ammunition. If the revenants broke through our metal storm, we were never going to make it to the MP5 ammunition.

So the motto when it came to bullets was "use it or lose it."

Most of our bullets never found their marks. Sometimes they struck the revenant behind the target, or they caught the target in the throat or the chest. However, that didn't matter, since the first impact stopped the revenant's forward momentum, and the second impact was more or less to the head.

While the bokor's powers were impressive enough to keep the dead mobile, even with a headshot, he didn't have enough brain power to guide each and every one of them to the target directly. He still needed the revenants to have a brain to process instructions.

We kept firing as they kept coming. There would be no remorse or stopping them. If we were lucky, one magazine would last long enough to bring down ten revenants.

We had forty magazines. They had a tractor trailer full of revenants.

Alex fired the M4, corralling the revenants into a tight cluster.

Then I opened fire with the Tommy gun.

Looking back on it, I couldn't tell you how fast we burned through all of the ammunition. But at the time, it felt like it took forever. We ran dry with at least three dozen revenants still out there.

Then a flaming dragon's foot came straight down on top of the small army of the undead.

Alex looked up, eyes wide. "Aw crap. Not again."

I smiled. Whoever operated the dragon had been so eager to get their hands on the bounty, he had sabotaged Baracus' little army. The dragon swiped down at the front of the house, sweeping away the entire front of the building. The operator wanted a clear field to get at us—either because he didn't want to chase us into the house, or because he was working in conjunction with another team. I couldn't tell.

I didn't hesitate, because I had already thought something like this would happen. It wasn't a trick you could only use once, especially if one could afford it.

Once again, in the middle of the flaming dragon was a small drone. I dropped the gun, swept down, and grabbed the fire extinguisher, and spun, hurling it at the drone. I fell into a crouch, picking up the Tommy gun.

As I expected, the fire was so hot, the extinguisher shell melted, spilling fire-retardant form all over. It briefly dispersed the fire construct.

Both Alex and I opened fire at the drone. It went down with little fanfare.

If all of these people were going to continue to get in each other's way, then we were going to survive this handily.

"Ha!" Alex barked. "Try throwing something else a little more difficult at us next time, assholes!"

At that point, with a wave of horrific stench, Rene Ormeno slammed into me, lifted me off of the couch, and hurled me to the back of the living room. I slammed into drywall, leaving a dent the size of my back in the wall.

Ormeno scruffed Alex, lifted him up off the floor, and through him the length of the living room, nearly to the other side of the house. Alex landed on a couch.

Standing in the doorway of the backyard to the living room, was Bokor Baracus. And Alex was on his own.

But so was I.

Chapter 21

CASTLE DOCTRINE

Alex started by opening fire into Bokor Baracus. He emptied his MP5 at full automatic, at point-blank range, into his stomach and chest. It should have opened him up like a zipper. The impact drove him back a whole one step.

When the MP5 ran dry, Baracus took a single long step forward and plucked it from Alex's hands.

He waved it at Alex like it was a toy confiscated from a naughty child.

"If you cannot be responsible with your toys, you cannot have them," he said jovially in his deep Jamaican voice. He flung it casually aside. Alex clamored up the length of the couch to escape the bokor.

Baracus continued. "I control all things that are dead." He raised his hand. "The epidurals of the skin? All dead skin cells. It is a simple matter to make them hard as armor when facing pistols."

"How about fire?"

Baracus laughed. "Still curious about how I escape from the fire pit when last we fought?"

"Kinda."

With a big grin, he said, "I don't feel like telling you."

Alex's eyes narrowed. He reached into his jacket pocket. "Well, let's see how you like this."

He hurled a clear plastic packet at Baracus. The bokor caught it easily. He studied its contents. He raised an eyebrow. "Did you just throw metal *dust* at me?"

"*Rust* dust. And magnesium. And aluminum tape." He shoved off of the couch, flipping over the arm of the couch. "Thermite."

The packet began to smoke, then ignited in Baracus' fingers. He cried out and leaped back from the fireball.

Alex hurled two more packets of thermite at Baracus. The flash powder inside set off each packet as it smacked against Baracus' chest. "Chemistry. *My* kind of magic."

Alex charged, pulling out his sidearm, jammed the muzzle of his gun into the bare patch burned away by the thermite. It fired three rounds into Baracus' gut.

The bokor shot forward and grabbed Alex's throat. He ground his teeth and growled, "You think bullets *alone* will kill me, little man?"

I FELL out of the wall, landing on my feet right next to the kitchen. I was dazed but still had my weapon. I raised it level with Ormeno. Ormeno grabbed it out of my hands and tossed it across the room, away from Alex and from me. It skittered along the floor of the kitchen, landing next to the oven.

Ormeno backhanded me across the face, twisting me around, and loosening three teeth. Just because he wasn't supernaturally strong when this close to me, didn't mean that he became a weakling.

Ormeno drove his fist into my stomach, doubling me over. He reached down to grab my hair and yanked back. His fist lifted over my head to crush my throat, and leave me to suffocate on the floor.

I pulled my folding knife and stabbed up into his elbow. Ormeno gasped and fell back, reaching for the knife. I held onto it as he stepped away. It yanked out of him as I fell to the floor on my hands and knees. I needed a moment to catch my breath...

Oh screw that, you don't have one.

I snapped my head around and locked onto his legs. I braced on my hands and my left leg, pulled my right knee up as far as I could, and kicked out. The sole of my foot drove right into his knee, bending it backwards. Ormeno screamed in pain and collapsed.

I scrambled to my feet and lunged for Ormeno, piling on top of him and driving my elbow into his face. Ormeno punched me in the ribs, bending them so hard they may have creaked. I grabbed his wrist and forced all of my weight down on his arm. I forced the arm down across his chest, pinning him to the kitchen tiles.

I looked into his eyes. He was angry. He was insane.

He was terrified.

Not surprising. He had, after all, had a small sample of hell. He had only started to grasp exactly what his life of depravity had in store for him.

"Repent, Rene. Before it's too late."

He ground his teeth and started forcing me back. "No. I would sooner face the endless fires of damnation than give you anything."

I growled, reared back, and struck him in the face with an open palm. "I." And again. "Said." *Thud* "Repent." *Crunch.* "Dumb ass."

Outside, more cars skidded to a stop outside.

Oh crap. These can't be on our side.

"Now!" I screamed for the microphones Alex and I had spent the day placing all over the house. "Now! Now! Now!"

This is where our real trap began.

Within seconds, the world filled with sirens and lights and gunfire. Helicopters swarmed in. Over at the shoreline, four coast guard cutters pulled up filled with armed men in full tactical gear.

You see, we had taken ADA William Carlton's advice. We had gone above the Mayor's head. We had called the state police and the Feds. And we didn't call on just the FBI. MS-13 wanted to kill me, so that brought in ICE and the DEA. Even though the higher-ups in Washington and Albany were as corrupt as you can get without being in New Jersey or New Orleans, the officers with boots on the grounds were always willing and able to arrest some bad guys and crack some heads. We had coordinated through the Staties and the Feds to come down at the last minute and close the trap on all of the hired guns the Mayor had brought after us.

Did I mention that, since the death cult had been shuttered, the surrounding homes in the cul-de-sac had been evacuated, sold off, and everyone had moved out? That's where the county and state SWAT teams had set up sniping positions. FBI's Special Tactics team had elected to move in from the opening of the cul-de-sac to cork the bottle.

In short, we had called in the cavalry.

BETWEEN THE LIGHTS AND SIRENS, and me having Rene Ormeno pinned, Bokor Baracus tossed Alex aside like a used handkerchief.

In two bounding leaps, Baracus slammed into me, knocking me off Ormeno. He grabbed Ormeno by the arm, hauled him to his feet, and promptly ignored him. Baracus' eyes were locked directly on me.

He reached into his billowing coat and drew forth a machete. "It is time for you to truly become a saint."

I reached back to the katana strapped over my shoulder and drew it out. "Bring it, necrophiliac."

"That is necro*mancer*."

"I don't care if you take them out for dinner and flowers first."

Behind him, Ormeno smiled and circled to my left. It was obvious this wouldn't be a fair fight.

A gun rang out. Ormeno torqued around and dropped. The bokor took a step back and looked to where the gunfire came from.

Alex stopped a few feet away, gun in one hand, paint bucket in the other. I had recognized the paint can. It was strangely made out of steel instead of the usual aluminum. And Alex had insisted on keeping it in a cooler filled with ice. "We weren't *done*, voodoo man."

I ran at Alex—okay, I ran *past* Alex—as he threw the paint can.

Baracas tried to bat the paint can away with his machete. It opened, spilling the green liquid contents all over him.

There is a chemical called chlorine trifluoride. To say that it is volatile would be like saying that Hiroshima endured high-speed urban renewal. It corrodes platinum and gold. It will ignite sand, glass; it will even set *asbestos* on fire. In the 1950s, there was a one-ton spill of chlorine trifluoride. It burned through a foot of concrete and another meter of sand and gravel below *that*.

It literally ignites with *air*.

Bokor Baracus, necromancer and Voodoo priest, went up in a ball of fire that filled the kitchen. It ripped through the oven, the sink, and the refrigerator.

The "smoke" coming off of him looked nasty, and I had a bad feeling about this. It was confirmed by Alex, who grabbed my arm and said, "Outside, now."

I didn't know why, but I didn't hesitate. We ran out through the living room as the walls, floor and ceiling started to bubble and smoke as well.

We made it outside, into the warm night air as the inside of the house turned into an inferno. I looked at my partner. "What the Hell was that?"

"As I said earlier, chlorine trifluoride—"

I shook my head and pointed at the inferno inside. The vapors coming off of Baracus had ignited the panes of glass in the windows. "No. I mean the smoke."

"Oh. That's not smoke. More like a cloud."

This had gotten frustrating. "Of. *What*?"

"Hot hydrofluoric acid. We should stay up here for a while."

"No kidding."

The world erupted in gunfire, and we hit the ground. The feds had hit the assassins, and the party had started without us. It was a good thing that we had called in back up because the cul-de-sac turn-around had turned into an armed camp while we were busy inside.

The various and sundry killers opened fire on the feds—with, among other things, literal fire. There were fireballs and lightning thrown around like hand grenades and footballs. There were RPGs from the street going for the helicopters. The helicopter had opened fire with a machine gun. The boats had opened up with machine guns. The state and county police had brought SWAT teams, and a pitched battle in the cul-de-sac had opened fire as well.

Alex looked on and winced as a helicopter took a fireball to the rear propeller. "Think we can help them?"

I grimaced. "Only if I bi-located into a SWAT team. I don't think I can do that. I could try, but—"

I smelled him before I heard him. The booming voice, like thunder, rocked the cul-de-sac, shook the ground beneath us, and rattled the surrounding windows.

"Enough!" it roared.

A wall of pressure slapped the helicopters out of the air and over the water. The swarm of assassins, sorcerers, gunmen, and whatever else had been parked in the cul-de-sac were pushed out of the street, through a house, and into the water.

Coming down the street, stomping like Raging Bull, came the warlock.

The team in the street spun around and open fired on him. He kept walking. The air thickened around him and bullets stopped, as though caught in foam, and fell to the ground. He kicked the used bullets out of the way and waved at the assault team. They all went flying into the bushes in someone's front yard.

The other homes in the area opened fire on him, and the warlock didn't even pay attention to them. He didn't care or didn't notice. The bullets kept stopping in the air near him. They were petty annoyances. He was unstoppable, and he knew it. He wouldn't let anything or anyone get in his way. Tonight was the night he paid his debts to his friends on the other side.

The warlock strode up to the part of the house that was on fire... and he leaped through the wall, into the kitchen, which was still a raging inferno.

He leaned forward and breathed in, sucking in all of the flames and all of the toxic fumes of steaming acid. The fire and acid were visibly sucked in through his mouth and nostrils like he was taking a breath of fresh air.

And then he laughed.

"Come in, Detective. It's safe now. We need to talk."

Mayor Ricardo Hoynes had arrived and had brought all Hell with him.

Chapter 22

SAINTS ARE DEAD

I slowly rose from the ground. Now that the night had gone from a firefight to dead silent, I felt a little silly still being face-planted in the dirt. I still had the katana in one hand. That also felt a little ridiculous. I sheathed it again but took the sheath off of my shoulder. I held it in my left fist and figured that I was going to need it.

I still had my sidearm in my holster, as well as my backup piece, but bullets hadn't done anything to him thus far. The gun might help if I went melee with him. It was hard to block a bullet when the muzzle is against the skin.

Alex grabbed my arm. I stopped long enough to look back.

Alex shook his head. "Don't go."

I smiled at him. I knew this was going to suck. And by suck, I meant hurt like a bastard. Since this began, every villain had called me a saint, and all of my friends and family hadn't doubted the assessment.

But as I noted before, there is no such thing as a living saint. A saint, by definition, was someone who had made it into Heaven. All saints were dead.

As I walked to the French doors, one of the smoldering lumps on the floor near the Mayor changed color. It had gone from charcoal black to blood red. The color continued to shift back to a pinkish color before consolidating in a dark complexion.

It was Rene Ormeno. The powers the mayor had given him had allowed him to survive a fluoride fire and clouds of hydrofluoric acid.

This is going to suck.

I stood in the living room, just inside the doors. The mayor was in the kitchen there was a foyer between the two of us. I didn't think that was nearly enough distance. "So, Mayor Hoynes, what can I do for you?"

Hoynes smiled. "You can die."

I shrugged. I kept myself at parade ground rest, only with my hands on the sheath and the grip of the katana. "I'll have to get back to you on that."

Hoynes gave an oily politician's smile and stepped forward casually, easily. "What can I do to change your mind?"

"How about you tie something together for me," I told him. He stopped and blinked, confused. "I get that you have a death cult as a mechanism to feed your powers and pay off your debts to friends from the Other Side. But I don't get the whole thing with Rikers. Why would you unleash *thousands* of possessed inmates on the city?"

Hoynes threw his head back and laughed. It was a great belly laugh that shook the foundations of the house, and that wasn't metaphorical.

"That's easy! In fact, I'm surprised it wasn't immediately apparent once you knew what I was." He shook his head, as though he had heard a funny pun that was still horrible. "Part of it would be to tie up the NYPD and wreck the fire department. But most of all, power."

I arched a brow. "Power over a wrecked city?"

He shook his head. "No no no. It would never get that bad. But the threat would be never-ending. I would guarantee that. After all, 20% of the population are already dependents of the state. None of them will ever vote Republican—they might insist that fraudulent dependents actually go out and get jobs.

"Right now, this minute, the average street cop could close every store on any given city block, given all the petty laws that are outdated but never repealed. That isn't an accident but designed to give me control over what I can shut down—which is *everything*." He stepped forward, his face...contorting in strange ways.

"Through emissions standards, we control what kind of car you drive." He stepped forward again. "We control what you eat, because *it's good for you*. Via taxes, we control your money. We control what you drive, what guns we allow you. Your *dogs*. Your *healthcare*. How you raise your kids. Their education. We even control what type of light bulbs you can use."

He laughed again. "Ha! Medieval kings took a mere 10% in taxes and called it a *tithe*. Sales tax *alone* is nearly 10%, and income tax is *so* much more. Even term limits don't affect me. After all, there are so many useful idiots in the City's administration, the media, and the what did you call it? The Demoncratic party? Making it a Sanctuary city means that we have 20% of the population who are afraid to leave our protection.

"But I'm the good guy because I provide forms of gentle enslavement. Imagine the Hispanic ghettos, dependent on the government and unable to talk to anyone outside of your neighbors or unable to leave. A free people who can leave is antithetical to our control. And the word is *control*. Now, just imagine an *entire city* where everyone is scared to go outside after *thousands* of demon-possessed criminals are unleashed. Everyone is scared to go outside. Everyone depends on my good graces to stay alive."

I scoffed. I laughed. "Power? That's it? That's all this has been about? Petty political power over one city?"

"And seven *million* souls," Hoynes interjected. "You underestimate the lure of power. And power is the name of the game. My entire party seeks power entirely for its own sake. We are not interested in the good of others; we are interested solely in power. Pure power."

I rolled my eyes, not impressed. I managed to ignore how bad the smell was. "Just like every other thousand-year Reich."

Hoynes' eyes flared, burning red with literal fire. "*No*. Not like them. *We* know what we're doing. All the others were *cowards* and hypocrites. The Nazis and the old Communists came very close to us in their methods, but they never had the courage to recognize their own motives. They pretended, perhaps even believed, that they had seized power unwillingly. They continued to claim that there was paradise just around the corner.

"Bullshit. We *know* that no one ever seizes power and intends to relinquish it. Power is not a means; it is an end. One does not establish a dictatorship to safeguard a revolution; one makes revolution to establish dictatorship. The object of power? Is *power*."

I realized, whether he knew it or not, that he had more or less just quoted *1984*. "And killing me will allow you to keep this power?"

Hoynes smiled. "And so much more. You know why I'm telling you all this?"

"Because it doesn't matter, since you're going to kill me?"

Hoynes grinned. "Oh, more like if you don't die, nothing else will matter. Besides. I was just a distraction."

Rene Ormeno tackled me from the right like a deranged quarterback. His grip had wrapped around my arm, pinning it to my side. I couldn't swing the sword, never mind draw it.

However, I drew the sheath from the sword and swung it like a club, smashing it against the side of Ormeno's skull. It rattled him only a little. His hand wrapped around the sword I held as he drove me against the wall. He swung his forehead for my nose, but I cocked it to one side. He barely missed. It looked like the world's most awkward hug with his chin on my shoulder.

"Let go of the sword, *jefe*," he whispered.

I blinked and let go of it. There was no good reason for me to do so. I wasn't even conscious of doing it. I did it purely on reflex. He asked. I answered.

"Now, shove."

I did, pushing him away, and adding an additional kick to his chest. He fell back against a couch, rolled backwards over it.

Hoynes however, had levitated a couch and hurled it at me. *Crap.*

I ducked down and dove forward, rolling under the piece of furniture as it flew into the wall. Hoynes cackled and flicked his fingers at me. Pipes exposed by the fire in the kitchen ripped from the walls and came at me like spears. I waited a moment for them to come at me, praying my timing would be right, then dropped. They sailed over me and embedded themselves in the wall.

Hoynes bared his teeth and spread his arms wide...

The shadows moved.

Hoynes' shadow moved first, stretching out behind him like the unfurling of bat's wings. Then the shadow twisted and grew tentacles, spreading out along the walls.

"I *am* the darkness, boy," Hoynes crowed, the fire in his eyes bright enough to cast even more shows along the room. A shadow speared out from the floor and came for me. I twisted out of the way, striking it with the sheath. It wrapped around the sheath and snapped it. It batted me away, slamming me against the French doors.

"You can't defeat me!" he bellowed. The fire in his eyes flared so much, I feared they would shoot fireballs next.

A shadow tentacle spit out from the ceiling, peppering the area around me with shards of wood. I rolled away, my coat taking most of the damage. Three of them slashed open my forehead, ripping the skin from above my right eye down to my temple.

Guided by experience (like a demon shooting telekinetic projectiles at me relentlessly without stop), I didn't get to my feet but pushed off in a random jump. I was in motion, twisting in the air, as another shadow punched through a wall and speared me in the right shoulder. To my surprise, it didn't spin around and play in my internal organs like a laparoscopic tool but disappeared after striking.

Maybe they're only good for one shot? I pondered.

Behind Hoynes, Ormeno rose up and charged ...

For Hoynes.

The Mayor barely looked behind him. His hand shot out and grabbed Ormeno by the wrist. He raised Ormeno off the ground. "You *fool*. What do you think you're doing?"

Ormeno didn't even hesitate but struck out with his left hand, driving a fist for Hoynes' face.

Hoynes caught the fist without thinking.

Still Ormeno fought, striking out with a knee. It actually connected, but weakly, more of a tap than a hit. "If I go to Hell, I bring you with me."

"Silly, *pathetic* little man. I gave you your powers. I *gave* you your strength. I can take them away." The shadows came for Ormeno and took him by the wrists and ankles.

I got off the floor and scrambled for Hoynes, but more shadows spiked out of the floor, turning the rug into a sea of bear traps.

Hoynes growled more ferociously than any bear. "You want eternal damnation *now* instead of later, Rene? *Fine*," he spat. "It's yours."

Darkness came for me even as the shadows played make a wish with Ormeno's limbs. More shadows came for Ormeno, spearing down his throat and up between his legs. He gave the most horrific shriek I've ever heard, and I have literally heard the cries of demons. The shadows crawled along his skin, peeling his clothes off, peeling his skin off.

All the while, I kept dodging crap from the floor walls and ceilings.

Darkness. Shadows. I need light... You, Lord, keep my lamp burning; my God turns my darkness into light. With Your help I can advance against a troop; with my God I can scale a wall.

I leaped for the back of the couch and pushed off of it, diving for Hoynes, thirty feet away.

I reached the apogee of my arc ... and kept flying, the levitation kicking in like I somehow knew it would.

Hoynes whirled around and slashed at me, his fingers outstretched. Shadow darts flew at me, slapping against my chest, but I didn't feel them penetrate. I didn't care. I smashed into Hoynes, elbow first. My elbow snapped his head back, my two hundred pounds plus focused in one square inch of sharp bone met the soft fragile bone and cartilage of his nose. He reared back and shoved at me but merely twisted my body as I fell past him. I dropped into a roll, coming up at the shadow cocoon that had wrapped itself around

Ormeno. He was now a black writhing mass of darkness that wailed and gurgled.

God is perfect. God's Word is flawless; he shields all who take refuge in him. For who is God besides the Lord? And who is the Rock except our God?

I knew it was probably a bad idea and that it was going to suck, but I grabbed at the cocoon around Ormeno, my hands covered in my own blood.

The shadows recoiled against the touch of my blood.

I blinked, shaken. The shadows that lashed out at me had thrown things at me or had disappeared after cutting me. Even the shadow darts had struck my chest...but had dissipated against the blood on my chest.

I reached for the shadow binding Ormeno's right leg. It recoiled into the floor, cowering from the touch of my blood.

I felt the footstep behind me more than I heard it. I dove forward as Hoynes slammed his fist down where I had been a moment before. His fist punched through the floor. He ripped out a water pipe and wielded it like a baseball bat.

I rolled past the katana that Ormeno dropped, picking it up in my left hand as I came to my feet. I whirled, meeting the pipe coming in as an overhead strike. I pushed back against it and attacked in a backhanded swing. Hoynes blocked it with speed I couldn't believe. But it didn't matter, because I smashed my head against his—specifically, I slammed the right side of my face against him, the side covered in my blood.

Hoynes recoiled, screaming in pain. He scrambled away from me, passing even Ormeno. I lunged for him, katana held out for a left-side swing. He swung the pipe to block me.

My lunge didn't stop but kept going as I levitated at him. I dropped a knee for his face, making it a whole new level of flying knee.

I whirled at Hoynes, bringing the sword down in an overhead strike. The shadows moved and blocked it for him. It ripped the sword from my hand and passed it to Hoynes, who drew it toward him like he was a Jedi.

It didn't matter. *It is God who arms me with strength and keeps my way secure. He makes my feet like the feet of a deer; He causes me to stand on the heights. He trains my hands for battle; my arms can bend a bow of bronze.*

The shadows moved around me, gaining substance and form. I brought up my hands—mostly my left, since my right arm was screaming at me to stop abusing it in this fashion—and waved everything to come and get me.

You make your saving help my shield, and your right hand sustains me ... which is a good thing, since my *right is shot.*

Your help has made me great.

I burst to one side as Hoynes came in with the sword, flailing past my right side. *You provide a broad path for my feet, so that my ankles do not give way. I pursued my enemies and overtook them; I did not turn back till they were destroyed.*

I side-kicked into Hoynes' knee, causing it to buckle and making him twist. *I crushed them so that they could not rise; they fell beneath my feet.*

A shadow lashed out for me, and I swatted at it with my blood covered hand. It burned and pulled back. *You armed me with strength for battle.*

I spun in a left roundhouse as Hoynes spun to his right, bringing up the sword. His face ran right into my fist, with the combined force of both of our body weights. *You humbled my adversaries before me.*

Hoynes rolled like a log, back into the ruined kitchen. He scrambled to his feet. Backing away like that made me turned back to the shadows in the living room. They had coalesced into one malevolent, hulking pool of darkness. It reared back and roared like a tiger.

Then the ziplock bags fell at its feet. I realized what they were and hurled myself to the left before they detonated into giant fireballs.

The shadows didn't like the fire. The shadow creature's legs disappeared out from under it, consumed by the flash. It fell back into the living room, which was the one place it shouldn't have gone. More bags flew in on its chest, bursting into flame and burning a hole in the chest of the creature. It melted into the rug and slithered back to Hoynes.

The cocoon holding Ormeno melted away as well, revealing a ruined, headless stump of what used to be Rene Ormeno.

Alex Packard walked into the room with a swagger. "Don't like it when the odds are a bit more balanced, do you, buddy."

The last of the shadow darted into Hoynes, and he stood up, his spine ramrod straight. He chuckled. "You think that having two of you makes things easier on you? I don't think so."

I knew what he meant in a split second. The shadow matter had a limit effect on me. It could touch me for a few seconds. It meant that Hoynes' power as a warlock couldn't affect me, through the grace of God—exactly because of the grace of God. That's why he hadn't grabbed me or threw fireballs at me or even electrocuted me with lightning from his fingers.

Alex, on the other hand...

I held up my left fist to signal Alex to stop. I stepped between Alex and Hoynes, backing up closer to my friend. I made certain to put the couch between Hoynes and me. Some of his wounds were already healing—starting with his broken nose from earlier.

"You're missing the point, your dishonor." I slipped my hand into my pocket. "You came to pick a fight with me, remember?"

Hoynes smiled. "I remember. Your grace won't protect you from a good old fashioned beat down!" he roared as he rushed me.

I simply stood there and waited for him.

And I prayed.

You made my enemies turn their backs in flight, and I destroyed my foes.

Every step of Hoynes put a hole in the floor and shook the house.

They cried for help, but there was no one to save them— to the LORD, but he did not answer.

Hoynes roared, cracking windows three miles away and making my head pound.

I beat them as fine as windblown dust...

He kicked the couch, and it broke in two, sending pieces to both ends of the living room.

I trampled them like mud in the streets.

Hoynes reached up for the sword, and the katana flew into his hands.

The LORD lives! Praise be to my Rock! Exalted be God my Savior!

Hoynes leaped over a row of armchairs and flew for me, sword held high.

He is the God who avenges me, who subdues nations under me, who saves me from my enemies.

That's when I sidestepped and flung the rosary from my left pocket into his face.

Hoynes screamed like a normal man, swatted the rosary away from his face, and belly-flopped on the floor. Alex darted in, grabbed the sword, and pulled back.

"Don't mess with the Lord thy God," I paraphrased at him. "It never ends well."

Hoynes growled. Suddenly, he was a blur. He had called up all of his power, all of his reserves, and unleashed. He grabbed Packard's wrist and twisted it with an audible *crunch*. He chopped down on Alex's forearm, breaking that, then smacked Alex across the face, twisting him around on the floor. He grabbed Alex's lapels and hurled him into the foyer, next to the headless trunk that used to be Rene Ormeno.

Hoynes whirled on me and charged. He rammed his shoulder into me so fast, I didn't know what happened at the time. I went flying.

I made it three feet before Hoynes caught my jacket and pulled me in, smashing his nose with mine. He held me with his right hand and punched with his left, driving it into my wounded right side over and over again. My ribs snapped one by one, turning my side into a river of fire. He punched my right shoulder, dislocating it. He knocked into my hip, and something definitely shattered. My world became nothing but pain.

All Hoynes did was hit me, and he never went near my open wounds or the blood that had dribbled down my body.

After an eternity (thirty seconds), Hoynes scoffed and tossed me like a discarded candy wrapper. I landed in the foyer, next to Alex.

Hoynes leaped over the living room and landed about four feet away from us. "Well, well, what have we here? Two dead cops."

I reached over to feel Alex's pulse. He was still alive for the moment.

Hoynes kicked me in my injured side again. "So, how are you enjoying yourself? Saint? Feeling superior? Feeling holy? Feeling righteous?"

I ground my teeth and pulled myself onto my left side. I propped myself up. If this was it, then I was going to meet his eye. "Enough."

Hoynes narrowed his eyes. "I've barely started."

I growled and ground my teeth. I pulled myself along the floor, despite feeling like I had drills boring into my bones. I dragged myself to the stairs and forced myself up. I propped my back against the stairs, so I was at least close to being upright.

"No. Enough of this *saint* crap. *Saint*?" I spat at him. "*Prophet*? Like you even know the *meaning* of the word. What have I predicted? I can tell you Western Civilization is heading to the gutter. You can read that in the paper. That Christianity will rise again and crush demonic assholes like you, and everything you've supported your whole life? Read a book sometime, it's what we do."

Hoynes took five steps and was over me. He placed one foot on a stair level with mine and leaned in. "Oh? And what will stop me once you're gone?"

I rolled my eyes, even that felt like it hurt. "Like God needs me to take you out. Evil overreaches and crushes itself. It's your nature. You always lose in the end. If nothing else, time will do it."

Hoynes grabbed my chin and forced me to focus on him. His demonic fires poured into my eyes. "Listen to me, little man. I have been here in many guises for many years. Centuries. I was here back when your grandparents were not even dreamed of. I lasted on dribs and drabs of power, killing those I needed for a few more years of power."

I blinked, confused for only a moment. "You couldn't kill fast enough, could you?"

Hoynes smiled. "Yes. You see? That wasn't very hard, was it? I was tempted to move to Europe. Then I founded the Women's Health Corps, and I had more power than I knew what to do with. How do you like that? Prophet?"

I channeled all of my rage into the roar that erupted from me. "*Enough! Fuck* you and your *saint*. And your *prophet*. I'm not a prophet of the Lord. If I were a prophet of the Lord, you think I would have spent my time fighting you? You think I would have gone through all this trouble? I'm an okay human being who hopes to one day get to Heaven. Maybe take care of my family while I'm at it. If I were a prophet of the Lord, you stupid sack of crap, then let fire come down and destroy you and *all* of your men."

Hoynes smiled and shook his head, entertained. He opened his mouth to gloat once more ...

And then we both heard it. It was a faint, far away whistle. It was like the sound of a cartoon bomb. The sound got slowly and surely louder as the source came closer.

I then realized that I might have gone a step too far.

Without any warning, I delivered a left jab straight up, into Hoynes' crotch. It wasn't a simple tap strike. My knuckles hit his pelvic bone.

The whistle was louder.

God. Please. Now, were the only coherent thoughts I could piece together.

I shot up off my back and levitated straight for Alex. I scooped him up in my good arm, and sped directly for the French doors. The whistle was loud and unbearable.

We crashed through the doors and into the backyard. We dropped into the dirt near the bushes at the back. We were only a few feet from where they once had the giant statue to Moloch.

Then a fireball as big as the house smashed into the former home of the Women's Health Corps and blew it up. The wreckage flew fifty feet into the air as a geyser of fire ripped it all to pieces and sent it flying. The various and sundry parts hovered in the air, as though suspended, for only a moment, but came crashing back down to the Earth.

Alex and I stayed perfectly still for a long, long time, settled in and ready to pass out.

"I think I may have overdone it," I said to the night sky.

Alex laughed, then groaned in pain. "Nah. It's just about the right temperature to deep-fry his ass."

I laughed. It hurt. "Okay, Lord. You win," I told him. "I'm convinced."

You exalted me above my foes; from a violent man you rescued me. Therefore I will praise you, LORD, among the nations; I will sing the praises of your name.

The wreck shuddered, and I didn't give it any attention, until it sounded like a very familiar pattern.

It was someone clearing away wreckage. *Aw crap. Dear God, give me a few more minutes of mobility, and I'll see what I can do about killing this son of a bitch.*

Mayor Hoynes smashed through the rubble like Superman buried under a building. He came down with a crash, landing on his feet only three meters away from us. He gasped for air, out of breath. Digging yourself out from underneath wreckage like that must have been difficult.

"You think ... that ... will stop me. I was in the Great Chicago Fire. Hell ... I *started* it. This ... is ... a ... camp fire."

I had a sinking feeling in my gut. We were out of ammo. We were out of steam. We were technically out of backup. My ribs were broken. I would never walk right again.

We were toast.

God. Let us not go down without taking him with us.

Hoynes straightened, took a step, and froze. He strained to lift his back foot, but it wouldn't move. He tried to pull back his other foot, but it wouldn't move either.

In the brightly burning flames from the house, Hoynes' shadow had grown huge.

And Hoynes' shadow bent around, towards the burning wreckage, and held Hoynes' feet in place.

All around us, the shadows began to move and come alive. They screamed with the shrillness of a thousand nightmares. They broke loose from their moorings and reached out.

Hoynes held up his hands. "No. No, you can't do this to me. Not *now*," he screamed. He pointed to me. "Your payment is right *there*. Just let me go. I can deliver him to you."

The shadows wrapped around his arms and legs, much like they had with Ormeno only minutes ago. They slid around his arms and legs like the darkest, sketchiest, tentacle hentai I could imagine. They covered his hands and feet and slid over his skin like living oil.

The monstrosities and horrors that had been after us at Hoynes' bidding had turned on him.

"Always feed your pets, Rickie," Alex scoffed. "Hungry dogs know no loyalty."

Hoynes began to scream. His cries went up in a wail as the living shadows crawled up his legs and disappeared into his pants. "No. Not that! Not that! *AHHHHAHHHHHHHHHHHH.*" The screams went on until the shadows skittered and slid into his mouth and poured down his throat.

Hoynes fell forward, and the shadows dragged him, kicking and gurgling all the way back into the house fire. Straight into Hell.

I looked at Alex and shrugged. "The Wages of Sin. I guess that's what happens when you don't pay your power bill on time."

Packard shrugged. "Eh. I thought that's what happens when you don't pay your exorcist bill. You get repossessed."

I groaned in pain. That joke was as bad as all of my ribs being broken.

Chapter 23

DEVIL'S ADVOCATE

"So, Detective Thomas Nolan, you've only killed the mayor, a score of cops, rampaged through two rich communities, angered two entire minority communities, and you've also disposed of the Deputy Mayor. Give me one really good flipping reason why you shouldn't be thrown into the deepest darkest cell in Rikers and see if you survive the night."

The acting Mayor was a gay bastard...so much so that it had been part of his campaign slogan when he ran in the primaries against Hoynes. Hoynes had won in a landslide, despite acting Mayor Lawson being gay, black, and "underprivileged" (defined as having no father, but waltzing through schools on minority quotas and lazy teachers, and getting into Columbia on the strength of a "Why Iran is the best country on Earth" essay—that was the actual title).

The mind boggled to truly wrap around the stupidity being thrown around so casually. Despite having been beaten and stabbed to within an inch of my life by the forces of Hell, I think this stupidity was actually getting on my nerves even more than Hoynes ever had.

Threatening to throw me—not Alex, not D, no one else but me—into Rikers was insane. Especially since I was in a wheelchair, half-wrapped like a mummy. My arm was in a cast, my ribs were wrapped, my hip was bad enough that I might not walk straight ever again. And this idiot thought to throw me in jail?

What a moron.

However, I had to give him this—the smell of evil had been purged from City Hall. Without Hoynes and Baracus, the scent that had made me sick to my stomach had dissipated. There was some lingering stench here and there, but I had assumed that came with politics in general.

While I let the threats roll over me, Mariel was nowhere near as amused. She had been the one to wheel me in. Given what had happened with the previous occupant of the Mayor's office, she wasn't going to let me alone while I was anywhere near City Hall.

My wife stood up, leaned over the desk and grabbed the acting Mayor by the lapels. She dragged him forward and said, in a low, deadly whisper, "Listen to me, you sniveling little bitch. My husband nearly *died* saving this city from horrors you can't even *imagine*, and you're going to threaten to throw him in *jail*? Are you insane!"

Lawson pulled Mariel's hands off of him. "How dare you insult my being gay!"

Mariel blinked, furrowed her brow, and cocked her head to one side. She looked to me and asked, "He's gay? Since when?"

I shrugged with my left shoulder. "It was in the primaries."

Mariel rolled her eyes. "Like I care who Demoncrats nominate."

"Madam! If you please!" he shrilled.

Before the screaming match could continue, the door burst open. In strode Father Richard Freeman, in full church regalia. His black cassock was trimmed in red, with matching buttons, a purple sash around his waist. He looked annoyed.

Freeman, however, didn't look nearly as pissed off as the man with him. It was a Eurasian gentleman I didn't know. He had deep black hair, wearing a dark, midnight blue FBI windbreaker that strangely enough, matched his eyes. For some reason, he looked vaguely familiar, though perhaps he just had that kind of face.

The...odd-looking FBI agent looked at Lawson like he was going to whip out a gun and open fire. "You! Are you Lawson?"

The acting mayor stood up as straight as possible. "Yes? And you are?"

"The guy who's going to kick your ass up one side and down the other."

Lawson sneered. "How offensive can you be?"

Father Freeman closed the door behind him as the Fed stormed forward, past me, and slapped his hands against the desk. He leaned over into Lawson and growled. "I'm going to offend you so hard, you're going to shit your pants."

I looked over my shoulder at Father Freeman. "Where did you pick him up?"

Freeman stopped over my left shoulder. "I was waiting in the lobby when he stormed through. I just followed."

Mariel was on my right and laid her hand on my good shoulder. "I like him."

Lawson rolled his eyes and glared at the newcomer. "May I ask what you're doing here?"

"I'm here to *hopefully* talk you out of being a total idiot."

Mariel laughed. "Too late."

"Because, seriously, how stupid are you?" the Fed asked. "Do you have any *inkling* of what would happen if news of last night got out? Does the term *riot and blood in the streets* mean *anything* to you? You flaming moron!"

"How dare you reference my sexual preference."

The Fed blinked, looked him up and down, and said, "You're gay?"

Father Freeman gave a polite little cough. "If I may interrupt...?"

The Fed threw his hands up in the air, backed away from the desk, and waved Freeman forward.

Freeman stepped forward and nodded at Lawson. "Hello. I'm from the Catholic Church, and I'm here to help ... Detective Nolan, not City Hall."

Lawson scoffed. "Sure. Like you can help this homicidal maniac who killed a SWAT team and two city officials."

Mariel huffed. "They were only politicians."

Freeman merely gave a small smile as he tolerated all of this. "You see, the Mayor, who while he claimed to be Libertarian, ran on the Democratic ticket. Your ticket."

Lawson rolled his hands in the air, indicating that Freeman should speed up. "And?"

"As such, that makes him the face of your party."

"Yes. So?"

The Fed growled. "Did you know that the FBI had wired the house and grounds of last night's shootout?"

Freeman smiled and waved at me. "By our request."

Lawson's face dropped, which made me wonder how much he knew about Hoynes' various and sundry practices. Had Lawson been a knowing lackey? Or had he just suspected? Since there was no stink of evil from him, I suspected the latter.

Either way, the color drained from his face, which was an impressive feat for him. "But, but ... but the house was destroyed," he stated confidently, his spine firming up. "You can't have anything left."

The Fed sighed at the stupidity. "All the footage was uploaded to an off-site server, in real time."

Freeman smiled. "You can't even imagine what the Mayor confessed to during the fight. Up to and including deliberately manipulating illegals, minorities, and trying to turn the city into a police state of willing slaves. Would you like to discuss prosecuting Detective Nolan now?"

Lawson blinked. His jaw tightened and ground together. His mind spun, racing for a solution. "Given the number of cops he killed, can Nolan really even stay in the city? There was even a cop killed in his own precinct, wasn't there?"

I sighed, thinking back to Mary Russell. It was heartbreaking to think that one of my colleagues could have even thought of taking a shot at me. Heck, I thought we had been friends before she leveled the shotgun at me.

"No," Freeman said, surprising even me. "And it is less because of the corrupt cops he has killed but because there is still a bounty posted for the Detective on the Dark Web."

I winced. *Yeah, that'd be a problem.*

Lawson blinked, confused that there would be a legitimate reason to fear for my safety. "But the mayor is dead."

The Fed growled again. "I have no patience for this idiot." He pushed past Father Freeman and slammed both hands on the desk to get his attention. "Look, moron, you can't just remove a page from the Dark Web and hope that's it. To find the page you're looking for, you need the exact URL. You can't just google *cop wanted dead or alive.* There's no way to be certain that all of the pages Hoynes posted the bounty on will be wiped. It'll take weeks, if not months, for all of them to be caught and scrubbed. Just because the mayor is dead doesn't mean that he didn't make an automatic payment system set up in the event of his death. It doesn't guarantee that everyone in on the bounty hears the announcement that the person who commissioned it is dead."

Freeman nodded. "We are also not counting the corrupt cops he foiled. They must be cleaned up and disposed of."

Lawson grinned. "So, he's gone. Disappeared from the NYPD. Maybe witness protection is in order, hmm? Send Nolan off to some nice little farm in Ohio."

The Fed sighed. "I think you mean Iowa or Idaho, dimwit."

Lawson gave an amazingly limp-wristed wave of his hand. Seriously, was he *trying* to be a stereotype?

"No," Freeman corrected him. "However, I do feel as though a transfer is in order. A transfer, perhaps, to the Intelligence Division? I am aware that the NYPD is the only department in the world that has its own foreign intelligence branch."

Lawson frowned. "I would have to talk to the Commissioner about that."

I didn't say *But you had no problem condemning me to whatever death you could arrange without talking to him.* I merely smiled and wondered if schadenfreude was a sin.

Freeman smiled. "I already did. He's all for it. I'm so glad you agree. We'll be going now."

Lawson opened his mouth, and the Fed held up his hand. "Oh no, you're letting them go. You and I still need to have a very long talk about exactly how stupid you are."

Mariel wheeled me around, and the three of us started for the door. I touched the Fed on the arm. "Is there a section of the Bureau dedicated to this?"

The Eurasian with the midnight blue eyes smiled. "Just me. I'm usually enough. Have a good vacation, Detective Nolan."

We wheeled out. The door closed behind us, and the shouting started a second after.

Praise be to my Rock! Exalted be God my Savior! He is the God who avenges me, who subdues nations under me, who saves me from my enemies. You exalted me above my foes; from a violent man you rescued me. Therefore I will praise you, LORD, among the nations; I will sing the praises of your name. He gives his king great victories; he shows unfailing love to his anointed, to David and to his descendants forever.

"In six months, the baby will have been born," I said to Freeman.

The priest smiled. "Oh, we can make arrangements around that."

Mariel gave a sigh of relief. "Thank God. I don't want to be entirely alone with my mother as I get huge."

"Amen to that." I looked at Freeman carefully. "So, where exactly are you sending me? Once I'm healed up, of course."

Freeman casually shrugged. "Oh. Certain people in Rome would like to talk with you. A very, very long talk."

ACKNOWLEDGMENTS

As we close out the first part of the Saint Tommy, NYPD series (no, this is not the end), I would like to thank some people I have missed in previous novels, as well as thank those who contributed to this novel.

First and foremost, my editors. All three of them: Margaret and Gail Konecsni of Just Write Ink, as well as L. Jagi Lamplighter Wright.

I would also like to thank Larry Correia, and his gun club with a book problem for the various and sundry advise I've gotten for these books. The ballistics of a nine millimeter in book one, the right age for gun ownership, all written with input from several corners of the internet. All mistakes are mine. But for someone who has held a whopping four guns during three range visits, I'm doing pretty darn awesome.

Also, this book is the culmination of suggestions from Hans Schantz, and my friend Jason. Hans suggested the development of abilities, and Jason suggested who the ultimate villain should be.

Of course, I would like to once again thank you, the reader, for joining me on this journey with Tommy Nolan. I'd ask that, no matter what you thought of the novels, you please go onto Amazon and/or

Goodreads, and drop a review. Hopefully, sometime soon, you'll have the opportunity to vote for *Hell Spawn* in the Dragon Awards.

Assuming you don't have another book of mine in the queue, you can find my ramblings on DeclanFinn.com, or find me on Twitter at DeclanFinnBooks.

Be well all. And God Bless.

ABOUT THE AUTHOR

ABOUT
DECLAN FINN

Declan Finn lives in a part of New York City unreachable by bus or subway. Who's Who has no record of him, his family, or his education. He has been trained in hand to hand combat and weapons at the most elite schools in Long Island, and figured out nine ways to kill with a pen when he was only fifteen. He escaped a free man from Fordham University's PhD program, and has been on the run ever since. There was a brief incident where he was branded a terrorist, but only a court order can unseal those records, and really, why would you want to know?

He can be contacted at DeclanFinnInc@aol.com

Follow him on Facebook and Twitter @DeclanFinnBooks

Read his personal blog: apiusmannovel.blogspot.com

Listen to his podcast, The Catholic Geek, on Blog Talk Radio, Sunday evenings at 7:00 pm EST

ALSO BY DECLAN FINN

SAINT TOMMY, NYPD

Hell Spawn

Death Cult

Infernal Affairs (forthcoming)

LOVE AT FIRST BITE

Honor At Stake

Demons Are Forever

Live and Let Bite

Good to the Last Drop

THE PIUS TRILOGY

A Pius Man

A Pius Legacy

A Pius Stand

Pius Tales

Pius History

ALSO FROM SILVER EMPIRE

THE PRODIGAL SON

by Russell Newquist

War Demons

Spirit Cooking (forthcoming)

LOVE AT FIRST BITE

by Declan Finn

Honor At Stake

Demons Are Forever

Live and Let Bite

Good to the Last Drop

PAXTON LOCKE

by Declan Finn

Hell Spawn

Death Cult

Infernal Affairs (forthcoming)

PAXTON LOCKE

by Daniel Humphreys

Fade

Night's Black Agents

Come, Seeling Night (forthcoming)